Attic.doc

The Oaktown Series

Attic.doc and *Days of Daisies* celebrate their characters' sexy queer lives. Over the course of one year in Oakland, California, they dive deep into themes of death, identity, and belonging.

See oaktown.dagmarmiura.com.

Attic.doc

Teja Rhae Watson

¶

DAGMAR
MIURA
LOS ANGELES

Published by Dagmar Miura
Los Angeles
www.dagmarmiura.com

Attic.doc

First published 2025

ISBN: 979-8-89195-061-0

WINTER

Thursday, January 7, 2010

Kamakura, Japan
11:22 a.m.
I can't feel anything. The Vicodin makes a big peaceful-
ness. Everything smooth and quiet, like yesterday never
happened.

My fingers glide around the keyboard like ghosts.

Twenty-ten, huh. Half of itself. How appropriate.

1:15 p.m.
In the bath just now, I did a butoh dance in my head. My
face was white, my mouth a red heart. Bouffant geisha
wig, gray kimono. There was a red bird on a sakura branch
above me, and I wanted to catch it.

From there the dance became a farce. How far away
what we want always is—a dance for those of us who never
even get close.

I shook the tree, knocked the blossoms onto the stage,
into the tub. I tripped on my kimono, splashed around in
the petals. I pulled the geta from my foot and flung it at
the bird, missed by a mile.

4:43 p.m.
Clara suggested that I should journal, to help me get
through this, since I'm alone. Just me and my new ruby-
red MacBook, which I bought with the money my parents
sent for Christmas.

No partner. Sean's away, like always. He's never here
when I need him.

No job. I can't go back up to that classroom. I can't see

the fear in the kids' faces. Haruka wouldn't fire me, but she wouldn't support me either. I bet she spent all day cleaning the rainbow rug—that's probably why she canceled school today. The rug cost 100,000 yen, but I'll be easy to replace. The shiny new *gaijin* will be lining up all the way to the Enoden station for the beautiful apartment, beautiful boss, beautiful kids.

No home. There's no way I can be down here, after what happened in the classroom, directly above my head. Hearing the kids up there. I can imagine them calling down to me—they know I live down here. There would be no hiding, no pretending everything is fine.

No friends. Clara offered to come over with Yuki, but that would have been too much. And Ai is no longer an option. Man, I wish I could call her right now.

No little seahorse. All of that is over now.

It's just me and the laptop. She needs a name, if I'm going to tell her all my secrets.

Sadie. Sexy Sadie.

Just you and me now, Sadie.

7:12 p.m.
I've decided the only thing I can do is leave. It's not the "right" thing to do, but where has doing the right thing gotten me? Deeper and deeper into this hole, till I can barely see the light.

Staying in this apartment is not a possibility. I won't survive it.

What happened upstairs yesterday—these things don't happen here. I'm messing up the perfect picture. I feel like a drag queen in a diorama, giant platforms crushing the temples and shrines of this ancient place, mascara dripping like tar all over the perfect stone paths. The King Kong of Kamakura.

I have this one chance to escape. Before Monday, when the kids will be back at school and Sean will be back from his trip. He wouldn't let me leave. I can't stand the thought of being stared at and worried over right now. Under the microscope, pinned under a slide like I've been stuck behind these plate-glass windows.

I'm sick of living in a display case. I'm suffocating in here.

I can go somewhere no one knows me and be only who I want to be. Who hasn't dreamed of that? I won't have to worry about being a good girl, being watched everywhere I go.

I can be queer again.

8:18 p.m.

Haruka called to tell me preschool will be back in session tomorrow, rather than Monday. Just like her to move right along—God forbid we should take Friday off to honor this loss. Nope—nothing to see here, folks. If she ignores it, pretends nothing happened, she won't have to deal with it.

I won't be teaching tomorrow, though. She assumed I would be, didn't even ask if I was up to it. She doesn't care about me. She may be my sponsor, but caring for me was never part of the job.

I told her I can't teach tomorrow, that I'm not well. But I didn't tell her that I'm leaving for good. I have to take care of myself now. I can't risk anyone trying to stop me.

The kids will come back tomorrow, the classroom will be spotless, Haruka will be her usual *genki* self, and what? They'll think they imagined the whole thing.

There's no way I can be in the apartment when the kids are here. So I need to be out of here by 7:45 and stay out till 5:30, after they've been picked up. Which means I have to be okay enough in the morning to go out, and stay out.

Fuck! Right now I feel like I've been picked up and wrung out. Like the goddamn rainbow rug.

Friday, January 8

3:34 a.m.

I just woke up, my shirt drenched with sweat. It was exactly a week ago that I woke up, at the same time, on the kitchen floor. I was soaked then too. Broken glass all around me.

I can't stop shaking. Everything hurts. My fingers are so cold I can barely type.

Breathe, baby, breathe.

Okay. I took a Vicodin. Changed into Ai's Depeche Mode shirt and a sweater, fingerless gloves, scarf around my neck to keep my sweaty hair off me.

I brought the laptop back into bed with me. Sadie, soft scarf, and Vicodin are what I have to get me through this.

Cold concrete at my back, cold even through my clothes. Cold floor under my futon. Cold fucking country.

What if someone finds a way in. A way to keep me here.

Think about being on a plane, flying somewhere warm. In just a couple days, you'll be done with this sad alone life. You just need to get yourself on a plane, and you can collapse when you get where you're going. We'll find a place where you can do that.

Right, Sadie? It'll be like nothing ever happened. That's what everyone wants.

Sleep, sleep, back to sleep. So you can get up and out in the morning. You need your strength for your escape.

2:20 p.m.

I'm writing at the café by the train tracks. The only place I could bear. At least I can have coffee. Best coffee in Kamakura.

I spent the morning with Daibutsu—the Great Buddha,

a 43-foot-tall bronze statue that I'm proud to call my best friend. I got up way too early, put the Vicodin and my laptop in my backpack, snuck out before the kids arrived, and took the train to Kotoku-in.

Daibutsu had a cute little hat of snow on his head. I sat at his feet, bundled in my down jacket, soft scarf, and mittens. I wished I could climb in his lap for a nap, like Mei on Totoro.

I'm going to miss him so much. I've been to see him at least once a month, for the four years I've lived here. That's like 50 visits. He was my therapist, my medicine man.

He's been sitting in the same place, meditating, since 1252. Nothing can break his concentration. I meditated with him today, his base at my back, tried to let him put things in perspective. Let the Vicodin kill my pain.

I asked him to help me figure out where to go. I miss California, but in S.F. and L.A. there are too many people I don't want to see.

And then I saw it, in the sky above Daibutsu: the red neon of the Fox Theater flashing OAKLAND, OAKLAND, OAKLAND. A shared space, with women, somewhere quiet and comfortable. I can hide out for a while, get better.

Finally I got too sore, sitting on the concrete. I got up, stood on my tiptoes, and put my head to Daibutsu's feet. Then I realized that I was saying goodbye, that I probably won't ever see him again.

Trying not to cry, I started to hyperventilate. I walked away from the tourists and ducked under the trees, by the stream. I sat on a rock and took another Vicodin. Once I was sufficiently numb, I emerged from the leaves and took the Enoden to this café.

On the way here, I was remembering another time on the Enoden, coming home from the yarn store. I was trying to unwind a skein of yarn I'd just bought so that I could knit with it, but I didn't know what I was doing, and it was getting all knotted. An older Japanese woman sitting across from me reached out, and without a word she showed me how to spool it into a ball, the red-and-black lambswool moving back and forth between us. The two of us shy together but connected by our shared task, by the softness of the wool.

I wouldn't let myself cry, thinking about this on the train, not wanting to attract any more attention to myself than I already do. I cast my eyes down. The Japanese are so polite, they will never let you see them staring at you. So the polite thing to do, in return, is to not see them.

Made it here, used the bathroom. Took my shoes off and I'm sitting on my favorite couch, my jacket under me just in case. Forced myself to eat some soup.

I'll miss this spot, the sweet kids who work here and the art for sale and the excitement of the Shinkansen rushing by out front.

I'll miss the Enoden too. World's cutest train. When I came for my interview on the Enoden, this city seemed so charmed, like an anime dream.

I can't think of all the things I'm going to miss. My head feels like an obstacle course. Over and under, around, avoid.

I need to be gone by Monday. When I think of seeing Sean it's like there are bugs under my skin. He would never let me go. And I need to go. I can't be in that apartment anymore.

I just found this on Craigslist:

You know you wanna...   (North Oakland/Temescal)
$700 incl. utilities
...be barefoot in the backyard, picking veggies.

...make music and laughter most of the time.
...adore and adorn our gorgeous old Victorian with us.

Our peaceful, furnished attic space is open! In search of one lucky, lovely person to inhabit it. We'll take care of you when you're sick.

Respect and magic thrive in this house. Please be conscious, kind, and open-minded.

I saw the ad, and I felt excited. I actually did. Through the Vicodin and the pain and the fear I felt something like relief. I wrote to them just now, at the anonymized Craigslist address, and when I went to type my name, *Nara* fell from my fingers. It looked good sitting there, it felt right. A new me.

I can't believe I'm leaving Japan without seeing the city of Nara and the golden Nara Buddha, the biggest bronze Buddha in the world. There was a photo of him in my guidebook when I was planning our move here: seated, eyes closed, holding up one hand. I felt him beckoning me to come.

He's sat inside Todaiji Temple for 1,300 years, almost twice as long as the Kamakura Daibutsu, and weighs twice as much. All around the temple, and through the city of Nara, deer roam free. The Shintoists see the deer as messengers of the gods. Whole herds of deer, in meadows surrounding shrines, as many deer as there are people.

So many things I wanted to see. I have to let them all go.

Please let the attic work out. I'm focusing all my energy on this prayer to Daibutsu—the Kamakura one and the Nara one too. *Please let the attic work out.*

6:17 p.m.

Home now. I was relieved to find it quiet—no Haruka

waiting for me, no straggler kids waiting for late parents. I missed them entirely, which is what I wanted…but now it's sinking in, that this is it. I won't be able to say goodbye. I won't see them ever again, those little humans that I love.

Because I just bought a plane ticket. I'm leaving in 48 hours—taking off from Narita at 6 p.m. Sunday, landing at SFO at 11 the next morning. The nonstop flights were all crazy expensive, but there's just no fucking way I'm stopping in Seoul. I need to get out of here.

Good news, my bank has a branch in Oakland. I'm glad I save some these past few years. I have $13,011, after buying my plane ticket. Should be enough to live on for a while.

I started packing. Taking the three suitcases I came here with. Leaving a box of stuff with Yuki and Clara till I'm ready for it. They're coming over tomorrow night, Saturday, for one last night together.

No word about the attic rental, but they're probably asleep right now. All the way home—to the bank and the tea shop, on the Enoden, walking—I chanted, *Please let the attic work out.*

Life goes on. It has to. The only alternative is that it doesn't, and I'm not ready for that.

And who knows, maybe it'll be nothing but smooth blue skies from here on out. I'll be free.

I'm almost giddy at the thought. It feels like fear, a flight of energy rushing up from my thighs.

Saturday, January 9

10:26 a.m.

Heard back about the attic in Oakland—we're gonna Skype in a few minutes, at 5:30 p.m. their time, 10:30 a.m. here. I just took a Vicodin. The pain is bad this morning, and I'm still bleeding a lot.

10:53 a.m.

Lily has the happy, open face of a kid and a fuzzy Afro that was pulled back into two pigtails—Audre Lorde meets Princess Leia. Asha's like Arundhati Roy mixed with Lisa Bonet—small, with short hair and huge, serious Indian eyes, lazy lids behind her glasses. The two of them peered out at me, Sadie's red case framing their faces, the last of their day's sun behind them like a spotlight, like an ad for California. Seeing that light made me anxious for it.

We Skyped for twenty minutes. They told me a little about themselves. Lily is 27 and in nursing school. Asha is 28 and works at a women's shelter.

I told them a few things about me, got creative with some of the details, tried not to seem like a freak.

They showed me the attic. It's small but looks safe, like the perfect cozy place to chill for a while.

I told them I'll give them the first three months' rent when I get there Monday. They said they'll be there to let me in.

5:07 p.m.

Someone just rang my bell. I ignored it, and I guess they went away. Now I'm sitting in the dark, afraid to turn on the lights. The blinds are closed, and with the lights off we can all pretend I'm not home.

One more suitcase to pack. I need to make some food for tonight. Yuki and Clara will be here in an hour.

I just realized the grocery guy left our delivery out there. Maybe he's the one that rang the bell, though he never has before. I can't even remember what I ordered. Last week, another life.

Sunday, January 10

1:18 a.m.

Yuki and Clara just went to sleep in the bedroom. We dragged the other futon into the living room for me, because I want to stay up and write it all down. Clara was happy to hear that I've been journaling, and she agrees that the new laptop looks like a Sadie. I gave Yuki my old laptop, her little brother's been asking for one.

We had such a sweet night. Yuki made her okonomiyaki for me one last time, and Clara brought the good sake and some music. I told them I'm leaving, that I won't be in touch for a while—in case Sean tries to reach me through them, I don't want them to have to lie for me. They offered that I could stay with them, but we all knew that wouldn't work. He would go straight to Tokyo after finding me not here, and we'd be back where we started.

They understood. Or maybe they think that my impulsivity is certifiable and my decision-making skills deeply impaired, but they don't know what to do except be supportive. Luckily I am certain. At least there's that.

Clara cried. We drank our sake. I took my Vicodin. We hugged a lot. Enough hugs to last us a while.

When I first met Yuki, she never hugged—it was something she started to do after being around Clara for a while. When she first started hugging she was hesitant, she would hardly touch you, but now she gives good hugs. It's weird, all the ways being Clara's roommate changed her, here in her own country. She was the only Japanese woman I was able to get close to. Other than Ai.

When we used to go out in Tokyo, I imagined that from behind, on the street, we must have looked like a giant Oreo, a study in contrast, in balance—Yuki and me tall, with our dark hair and dark clothes, flanking small, light Clara, with her honey-blond hair hanging down her back.

When I got my cherry blossom tattoo, they held my hands. It was my first sakura season, Sean was away, and the three of us had gone to Ueno Park to hang out all day with the rest of Japan, drinking sake and making friends and celebrating the irresistible pink flowers blossoming all around us. I had been totally giddy, drunk and inspired, and when we saw a tattoo parlor on our way back to their place I pulled them in with me to get a keepsake of the day, around my belly button. I lay back on the table, eyes closed, head spinning, and they stood on either side of me and each took a hand, squeezing against what felt like knives cutting into my belly.

They took care of me last night too. My pain seemed smaller somehow, with them here.

I'd pulled out most of my clothes for them, and they put on a little fashion show for me—dressing in the bedroom, with the hallway to the living room as their runway. I lay on the couch, howling along with the Plastic Ono Band CD Clara brought me, especially "Mother," with all its *Goodbye*s and *Don't go*s. Mostly, though, I felt peaceful watching them, remembering our nights at their apartment in Tokyo. I had the happy thought that they will still be here together, best friends and roommates, that they will have each other for probably a very long time, and I realized that's what I want: what they have. The closeness of a close friend. Someone who knows everything.

We waited till around 10, when the food stalls on the beach would be closing and people would be heading home, and we walked down there, our sake in my pocket. They knew I was nervous about seeing my students and they flanked me this time, like bodyguards. Our balance was off, but it felt good to be protected. On our way we stopped at the *combini* and got wood and sparklers and a bunch of snacks I was suddenly very sad to be leaving.

We found a fire pit that wasn't being used and laid out our blanket. They bundled me up and made a little fire. I sat and snacked on Pocky sticks, *sembe* crackers, red bean buns…I wasn't hungry, but it felt like the right thing to do. Looking around, I remembered why I stayed so long. Bonfires on the beach. Dinner on the beach. Everything on the beach.

My gaze blurred and kids running by with sparklers became cars whizzing by on the ocean highway…. That was when I realized how high I was. Clara and Yuki came and sat on either side of me, holding me up. Yuki put her arm around me and pulled me back to a driftwood log behind us, and I settled into it, passed them the bottle.

Some kids at the next bonfire had music, and they were playing "99 Luftballoons," and Clara danced for me like she used to when we were kids, her braids flying, like she was Pippi Longstocking and the blanket was her bed.

I told them I have decided to become a butoh dancer. We all pretended to take my new career very seriously. They asked me to perform for them, I said I would if the right song came on. Meanwhile Yuki did her robot dance around the perimeter of the blanket, like the Tin Man.

We walked down to the water, holding hands. I thought how nice it would have been to have two mamas. I pulled off my clothes and handed them to my friends and then dove into the water in my bra and underwear, coming up with a grin so they wouldn't worry, then back under and away. It was cold, but the cold felt good. I wasn't worried about the animals under there with me. I felt them welcoming me back, to visit what I'd lost.

I did my butoh dance there. The ocean was my partner, holding me gently but firmly. I gave it up to her, let her move me, stretched my body out behind me and looked up at the stars. I waved at the waves as I moved up and over them. *Goodbye.*

10:47 a.m.

I fed Clara and Yuki tea and toast after they woke up, then gave them one last hug and watched them walk away from me. Down the path together toward the station with my box of stuff and their bags of my clothes, Clara's braids roughly intact from last night, the sequined butterfly on the back of my jean jacket flashing under the gray sky. It fits her perfectly, always was too small for me.

I miss them already, a new ache. It'll be hard to stay out of touch. Maybe someday they can come visit me in California. I won't be coming back here.

I leave in seven hours.

2:08 p.m.

I'm having leftovers. I don't have it in me to make some big final meal, and it doesn't get much better than Yuki's okonomiyaki. I'm still not hungry, but I'm making myself eat. Took a long bath earlier, let myself cry into the water. Definitely going to miss my fancy tub, but the new place has a clawfoot. In a clawfoot I can stretch out. Japanese tubs are not made for tall people.

Finished packing. Wrote Sean a letter. Now all I have to do is 1) call a taxi, and 2) breathe. I keep losing my breath. I have to actually stop, focus on bringing it back.

Four hours till I'm in the air.
Breathe, baby, breathe. You can do this.

5:44 p.m.
At the airport, waiting to board. I'm sitting on the floor with Sadie, burrowed in a corner so no one can sneak up on me.

I can see the plane, they're cleaning it now.
So close. Breathe.

I left my letter for Sean on the kitchen counter, locked the door and pushed my keys through the mail slot. Express-mailed Haruka a letter from the airport. It won't arrive till after I'm in the air. Closed down my email accounts so they can't write me. Opened a new email account and sent my parents a fake update that'll keep them satisfied for a while.

Once I'm on that plane I'm free. It'll be today there, when I land, even though it will be tomorrow here. Time's going to stand still for me.

Over the Pacific Ocean
Some in-between time
So far smooth blue skies, just like I hoped. Flying on Vicodin feels like really flying. I keep imagining I'm out there riding the clouds.

Nothing but ocean as far as I can see, and no one sitting next to me—a parting gift from Daibutsu. I even ate a croissant sandwich with egg salad, and it was actually pretty tasty.

I can't believe I did it. Me and you, Sadie. So decisive!
I feel bad about leaving Sean, but it was the only way.

He'll understand, someday. I hope. And if not, well, I had to do what was best for me for once in my life. I only have me to look out for now.

Sayonara, Daibutsu. I miss you already.

Sayonara to all the temples and shrines.

Sayonara, Yuigahama Beach.

Sayonara, beloved ramen shack, café by the train tracks.

Sayonara, children of Hikari International Preschool. I am so, so sorry.

Sayonara, quiet walking paths, flowers of every color.

Sayonara, Enoden, world's cutest train.

Sayonara, Onari Dori, the pet store with the parrot who says "Koooooonichiwa!"

Sayonara, dollar stores. I will really miss you.

Sayonara, bamboo forest.

Sayonara, sakura.

Sayonara, Ai.

Sayonara, Clara and Yuki.

Sayonara, Sean.

Sayonara, my sweet little seahorse.

Sunday, January 10

Oakland/Berkeley border, California
1:43 p.m.
I found the house by looking up. Lily said to look for the tallest palm tree. It's in front of me now, outside my window in the attic, stretching to the sky like my very own beanstalk. Lily and Asha said there's a raccoon family living in it.

The house is a pink Victorian. I laughed when I saw it. When I asked for a house with women, I didn't mean it should be pink!

Lily opened the door, that same light I'd seen on Skype beaming down on her from the window at the top of the stairs. She was barefoot and braless, in a sundress and hoodie, and she looked so happy to see me, I almost cried. She hugged me hello then helped me drag my suitcases up the narrow staircase to the second floor, then up an even more narrow staircase to the third floor. The attic is the peak, a place to stop and catch your breath.

Asha was up there, airing it out, and there was a breeze roaming through, and more of that good light. Looking into it is like a death wish. Life wish. Both.

I can see San Francisco and the Golden Gate Bridge from up here. They look like props in a set.

Asha left a prayer candle decorated with HAPPY HOME burning in the little altar alcove, set back in the eave above the stairs. She said the candle is most powerful if I let it burn until it goes out. I'll be around the next few days so I can keep an eye on it. She also left me a bundle of sage she made. She seems very serious, curious about me but guarded.

The last roommate left a bunch of furniture up here. A polka-dot armchair on the north side, by the window that looks out on the yard and the rooftops of Berkeley. Dark purple dresser and an old armoire with former roommates' tags carved into the side. A small bathroom with sink, shower, toilet.

On the street side, overlooking Oakland, I moved the desk to the window by the bed. I'm sitting here now.

For the first time it feels possible, the other life I've been dreaming of. Like I dreamed it into being.

I'm Nara now. I brought Nara here, to the border of Oakland and Berkeley. Exactly in between—the HERE and THERE sculptures up the block mark the spot, my taxi driver pointed out like a tour guide.

I need to write it all down, keep things straight. It's hard to think with all the buzzing in my head.

I told them:

1. I'm starting my MFA in Creative Writing at Mills in the fall (not true, but I needed a reason to be here)
2. I'm almost 30 (true)
3. I've been teaching preschool in Japan for the past few years (true)
4. I like girls (true)

I did not tell them:

1. That Sean exists, that I left him, that soon he will be getting home to find me not there
2. What happened on Wednesday
3. That I don't know anyone here or have any idea what I'm going to do next
4. That I'm hiding out in their home

That's not so bad, right, Sadie? It's keeping track of your lies that's the tricky part, they say. And lies of omission, I don't think they really count with new people.

They made my bed for me, a mattress nuzzled under the eave, soft red comforter and red gingham sheets. Across from the bed, in the altar cubby, the Happy Home candle beckons me to sleep.

7:18 p.m.
Slept for a few hours. Woke up to the end of the sunset, colors changing over the bay like an abstract painting, like something happening to someone else. It's dark now, the candle flame the only light up here. My head is clearer, the beehive has quieted. But it's still like a dream that I'm here.

When I was little, in Southern California, there was a white peach tree outside my window. Their flesh was a perfect thing that became even more perfect when broken.

In San Francisco, it was a redwood, heartening, grounded.

In Japan, it was the cherry blossom tree, polka-dotting the sky pink.

Now it's a palm tree, home to a raccoon family. A feral paradise.

January 11

4:55 p.m.

I slept most of today. The time that I lost en route is almost gone. Lily and Asha have been quiet, or maybe they're out.

Took a bath downstairs in the luxurious clawfoot, put on my kimono, brought Sadie into bed with me. The eave slopes just steep enough for me to sit up, like I'm framed by the roof of the house. Everywhere else in the attic, I can stand up with a few inches to spare. Plenty of room for my butoh, ha ha.

My very own space. It's perfect. I don't have to go anywhere or do anything. The Happy Home candle is still keeping me company.

Made myself some salad and tea and brought them back up. Lily and Asha told me to help myself to everything, we'll share food expenses. They're vegan, and the kitchen is full of good food, lots of vegetables, such a treat after the outrageously expensive produce in Japan.

It's windy outside, and the house's joints creak. I can hear BART rushing to and from Ashby station. Reminds me of the Enoden. Not as charming, but convenient.

Still taking the Vicodin. It slows everything down just enough for me to handle it. Smart drug. The pain is mostly gone, but every now and then a cramp hits hard. Best just to stay medicated.

Jet lag is like limbo. Like there's still a chance of going back. You have to choose to step under the rope, to the other side.

11:51 p.m.

Asha made curry and yummy coconut rice, to welcome me. So nice to have Indian curry again after the stew-like stuff in Japan. Asha's a good cook, her mom taught her when she was a kid.

Lily was playing music at a coffee shop in our neighborhood tonight, and she convinced me to go with them. I was wired after sleeping all day anyway. We walked the few blocks to the Nomad Café. It was cold out, colder than in Kamakura. Spooky too. Men in doorways, their eyes hungry on us as we passed. Lily and Asha walked on either side of me, insulating me, like Clara and Yuki had on our walk to the beach. Watching our back. It's been so long since I've had to do that—some say Japan is the safest country in the world.

Lily wore a black T-shirt with the sleeves cut off and a silver lightning bolt down the front, her 'fro pulled back pompadour-style, with long silver earrings. I met her boyfriend, Brix, who plays the drums. They've been together for a couple years, she told me, but tonight was their first show together. He's in a band with a friend of his from high school.

Lily looked completely at ease on the little stage, the sparkle in her eyes visible even from the back, where Asha and I were sitting. She smiled and strummed her banjo and sang songs about frogs like the world's sweetest rock star, and then she sealed the deal with a cover of Lennon's "Jealous Guy" and some excellent whistling. Brix joined in on the final verse, loose and easy behind his drums, propping her up.

I felt like I was melting. Whatever froze inside me these past few days, these past few years, dissolved into a cold pain in my heart. Lily is so bright it's, like, dangerous to look at her. But impossible to look away.

Where *am* I? I kept thinking. Could I really have landed, just perfectly, here?

Asha and I sat in the back with our beers, good, dark beer, such a treat after all the lager in Japan. We didn't talk much. She has a faint British accent, from spending the first half of her life in India, and that combined with the way she only half-looks at things gives her an air of being too good for everything, like we don't deserve for her to open her eyes all the way.

It's been so long since I've seen music in a café. Everyone looked so young, but they seemed so happy. In Japan everyone would have been trying to act cool. Here they don't seem to care. I looked around and saw that everyone else was fixated on Lily too, tattooed moths drawn to the earnest, vibrant flame.

She has what we all want: a clear path ahead. It's like she's exactly who she's supposed to be. Everyone else is a little dimmer, dialed down, next to her.

I don't even have the energy for envy. I just want to bask in her light.

This is all so unreal. Writing it down makes it feel like it's actually happening. Sadie's a big comfort in this new world.

I've never journaled before. Sean was always the writer. The words surprise me, emerging more from my body than my mind. Like when I realized I could read to my students and be thinking about other things. I'd be reading them a picture book before naptime and scheming about what I was going to cook on my lunch break downstairs—and suddenly find myself on the last page of a book I didn't remember reading.

Now it's midnight and I think I'm on the same schedule as the other humans around me. I guess it's time for sleep.

January 12

1:17 p.m.

Feeling more stable today, functional with caffeine. No Vicodin yet. There are only ten left, so I better save them for when I need them. The pain's pretty much gone.

I went down to the backyard today. Down the steep attic steps to the second floor. Past the guest room, Lily's room, their bathroom, Asha's room, through the living room and the kitchen, out to the sitting porch, down the back stairs. Carrots, onions, garlic, snow peas, greens. Roses and poppies. Plum, apple, lemon, fig trees. Wild weeds and grasses everywhere.

The house also shares a weekly CSA box from a local farm. Community-Supported Agriculture, straight from the farmers, new since I left. The box was delivered today— cabbage, carrots, celery, potatoes, leeks, spinach, oranges, apples, and persimmons.

Lily asked me to bring the box downstairs to divvy it up with and meet our downstairs neighbors, who live on the bottom floor of the house. Claudia is Argentine, in her late 40s, and has a daughter, Ingrid, who's 13, *pobrecita*. Ingrid's dad is American. Claudia said, "He insisted on this name, Ingrid, and then he took off."

She smiled sadly at her daughter, who looked embarrassed, and said, "I prefer Ingy."

They were so open with me, trusting me with all this personal info, it made me feel safe. Claudia is a single mama, works at a co-op bakery, wants to open her own.

Ingy is a total Japanophile. We talked about Miyazaki, she's seen them all. I told her she reminded me of a Latina Princess Mononoke, with her moccasin boots and ripped skirt, and she got all excited. "You just need some giant wolves," I said.

Claudia made bread with the persimmons, and we ate it warm from the oven, dripping butter all over their kitchen, grinning at one another.

I feel like I'm in heaven.

9:12 p.m.

There was a big earthquake in Haiti today, a 7.3. I went down for a bath and Asha was crying and watching the news on her laptop. Hundreds of people are dead, lost, without a home.

I've never lived somewhere that doesn't have earthquakes. All those big ones in Japan… It could happen here too, any minute.

Up here, looking down on the world, the attic feels like a fortress, like a watchtower.

But the roof could cave in at any moment.

January 13

3:33 a.m.

I dreamt of the kids just now. They were all swarming around me, all needing me, and I was trying to help them but then realized I couldn't and just sat down in the middle of them.

They started dancing around me, their little hands touching me like a maypole. Around and around they went, singing in Japanese, protecting me. Haruka was nowhere to be seen, blissfully it was just the kids and me, like I always wanted.

Woke up wet with sweat again. Nothing but Sadie to help me fight the night.

How long can I keep up this game of pretend? I'm playing house here, I'm playing with these sweet people. I'm hiding like a criminal.

I miss her. I miss having her inside me.

January 14

Up here in the attic, my Happy Home candle still burning, I feel like a lighthouse keeper, a puppet master. Pulling their strings with each click of a key.

I have a lot of time by myself in the house, while Lily and Asha are at school and work, and I wander through it, exploring—it's like a dollhouse, everything in its place. There's even an herb closet, the walk-in coat closet at the top of the front stairs, filled with dried herbs and tinctures and alphabetized, amaranth to ylang ylang. Lily gave me some ginseng and valerian to help with the jet lag.

I like to look at their things. I notice details now, so I can bring them up here, to Sadie. It keeps me from nodding off, slipping away. I have to record the life happening around me, get as much of it down as I can. I feel a responsibility, not sure who to—to me, I guess—to record this period in time. Like it might save me somehow.

Asha's room is painted teal, and it's dark, her one window covered with heavy brown velvet. An altar to Kali, an urn holding someone or something named Brownie. Candles of every size and color. A shoebox of tiny bottles of oils: Bendover, Black Panther, Sweet Pea. Pink protest signs propped on the crown molding—REPRODUCTIVE RIGHTS NOW, WOMEN SAY PULL OUT, IMPEACH THE SHRUB.

Lily's room is a warm sunny yellow, and her windows are always open, so it smells like the outside—feels like it too, with plants, feathers, rocks, bones, and branches everywhere. Her bed in the corner with its homemade quilt, scarves and necklaces trickling from the bedposts. Ferns and ivy gently casting spells, transplants leaning into the sun.

I started stroking a small white feather and it was so soft I couldn't let it go. I hid it under my mattress. She has lots of feathers, probably won't even notice it's gone.

In the living room is a print of Frida Kahlo in her *Self Portrait with Cropped Hair,* in Diego's suit with her shorn hair on the floor, Lily's thriving vines framing her. Asha told me it's the first self-portrait Frida painted after their divorce.

Freeda. She looks like she's winking at me.

January 15

I figured out why Asha's eyes don't open all the way. It's 'cause she's always stoned.

We hung out today in the attic and she got me high. She told me she's decided to be a lesbian. She's never been with a woman, but she's tired of wasting her energy on men. "Women are just so much more pleasant," she said in her lyrical voice.

"Word," I said. It's fun to use my slang again. "That seems like a logical, intelligent decision."

I think maybe she wants to flirt with me but doesn't know how. I don't know what I'd do if she did. She's beautiful, but I need someone more butch. Someone bigger, at least. Asha's a tiny person, I'd be afraid I'd break her. No matter how tough she seems.

She went to elementary school in India, but her parents moved to Chicago just before she started middle school. She's doesn't talk about her work at the shelter much. I guess she has to protect her clients' privacy. But she also just seems much more interested in figuring out how much of a feminist I am, whether she can trust me.

She asked what sign I am, and when I told her Taurus she said, "Ahhh," like it all made sense. "You're a good girl." She said Taureans are usually stable, law-abiding.

"Boring," I said. I didn't tell her that it's exhilarating to be unstable for once in my life.

"No, not boring. Easy. And sensual. You're the most earthy of all the signs."

She's a Cancer. I've never known a Cancer. She said, "We're known for our contradictions. Loyal and nurturing, yet moody...sensitive and intuitive, but afraid to trust."

The pot made me super chatty, and I told Asha about

Dani. That we met in film class at S.F. State. That I'd never seen anything like her, had been waiting all my life for her without knowing it. That she broke my heart.

"How?" Asha wanted to know.

"She wouldn't give me what I needed."

"What?"

"Love."

But oh, man, I loved her anyway. I remember the first time I told her. Moving above her, kissing her, then pulling back and looking down at her face and feeling, then saying, those three magic words. They were like a resurrection.

How fully we opened to each other, how brave we were. I can't imagine being open like that now.

I pulled myself back to the attic, where Asha was sitting next to me on the floor, one arm leaning on my mattress, looking at me. The candle she gave me was still flickering behind her, and I had no clue what she was thinking. Her eyes are a mystery.

She asked if I knew about Dani when I met her. If I had known I liked women.

I hadn't. "At first we were just good friends," I told Asha. "We used to cut film class and go to the movies instead. But then one day she called me on the phone, and suddenly something shifted. I just sat there, frozen, listening to her sweet voice, and I was like, *Oh, shit. I am in trouble.*"

I paused, not sure how much I wanted to get into with Asha. She nodded me on, practically panting like a puppy. I'd never seen her excited before, it was impossible to resist.

"A couple nights later, we were celebrating her birthday at this crazy strip club—"

"You went to a *strip* club?!"

"Yeah, but it's cool, the women have a collective." Asha looked half horrified, half mesmerized. "Anyway, Dani was getting a lap dance behind a curtain, right behind where I was sitting at the bar. I was feeling terribly jealous, and then she came out and I turned around. She must have seen it on my face. She walked over and spun my barstool around, straddled my legs to stand between them, and kissed me.

"We stayed up the whole night, and it was amazing, a million times better than I'd ever dreamed. In the morning I told her so, and she smiled her crooked smile at me, happy. I lived to make her happy.

"I was crazy about her, Asha. So crazy. I couldn't think of anything else. I wanted her so badly, all the time. We would kiss for hours."

Our kisses were perfect. They were like art. Like we were sucking on each other's souls.

I haven't wanted to think about this, all the time I was with Sean. I was scared to acknowledge the want in me. Now I'm afraid I won't ever find it again.

Asha wanted to know about the sex.

"I was naive about a lot of things, but she was patient with me, and she praised my efforts. The first time I went down on her, she said she didn't believe me that it was my first time. She was probably just saying that, but it made me feel good.

"Mostly what I remember is our skin together, how unbelievably good it felt, how undeniable. It created a very strong pull."

Asha's mouth was hanging open.

"I was so in love with her. Like, a scary lot. I would have done anything for her."

I looked at Asha and tried to imagine her feeling that way about someone. It came back to me, the egolessness of falling for someone like that. The willingness to fall even though there's no net to catch you. You have to want it bad enough to risk the hard pavement below.

That's how Sean loved me. With all he had, like I loved Dani. And I never was able to love him back in the same way, just like she'd never been able to really love me, because someone else had hurt her before I arrived. So I guess I know what it feels like, to be him. To be not loved right, and left behind.

I haven't heard from him, but then he has no way of reaching me. My mind wanders to him, alone and confused in our apartment, and I have to pull myself back to the attic, or it feels like I won't survive having caused that much pain.

It's like, after getting my heart crushed by Dani, my heart is too smart to let that happen again. So now all I can do is cause harm. I should probably just be alone, because this will probably just keep happening.

Asha was waiting for the rest of the story. The end was not as fun as the beginning, but I had to finish what I'd started.

"I know some part of her loved me too, even though she never told me. Now I think it scared her. That vulnerability. Pushing me away was easier for her than waiting for me to leave on my own. That way she could feel she had some control.

"So she kept breaking up with me. We were off and on for a while. I came every time she called—she was the butch and I was her loyal femme, she would give a little tug and I'd come running back. Until finally she ended it for good. I had just finished college, so I moved back to L.A."

Moony and I had moved in with Sean then, and he and I had gotten together soon after. I fell apart, let him gather up the pieces and try to put them back together. He never really stopped trying, and he never really succeeded.

But I didn't tell Asha that.

Sometimes it feels silly, these things I'm hiding. But I'm not ready to talk about what I left behind.

My butoh dance of the Dani breakup would be me mummified as she and Sean rolled me up and down the coast, yanking me back when the bandages reached their end. Nothing to do but rest where you end up after a dance like that. I ended up in Japan.

"I left for Japan a few months after that."

"Then how long were you in Japan?"

And suddenly I was saying "Three years." Somehow it sounded less psycho than four. I didn't think Asha would understand how I lost my free will there. Now here I am with nothing to show for it, hiding in an attic.

I'm afraid Asha can see right through me, to all the things I'm hiding. Probably she wants me to offer it up first. We're like hungry dogs circling each other, wanting more but afraid to be the first to pounce. The desire to lie down before her and let her devour me is hard to resist. I don't want to hold it together anymore, I want to lay it all before Asha, before Lily, have them look at me, see me.

But instead I hide under the covers. I sit at my altar and plead with the Daibutsus—the silver Kamakura Daibutsu on the right, and the bronze Nara Daibutsu on the left, two lions guarding my psyche.

Make me better, I ask them.

January 16

It never occurred to me that I'd have culture shock coming back to California. But it's scary out there, compared to Japan. After a few years, safety seeped into me. It was strange at first, I'd never really felt fully safe before. But then I too stopped locking my bike, stopped watching my back. I let all that go. And nothing bad ever happened to me there. Nothing I didn't bring into the country myself.

My problems were like spoiled food that I brought over, and now dragged back here from there.

Our next-door neighbors sit on the porch and bullshit all day, and it wafts up and into my window. Claudia said it's a crack house, which is why there are always so many people coming through.

I went out yesterday, to buy a cell phone. Sounds happen in the city, you can't expect quiet, but now they startle me. It's like I'm shell-shocked, like a soldier returned too late. I totally ducked and covered my head at the roar of a cargo truck's rear door being yanked down by its driver. So embarrassing.

Even though nothing bad happened out there, everyone I pass feels like a potential aggressor, or a potential person who knows Sean—like I'm in some video game fighting for my life, the hood over my head my only protection.

I need to get used to this place, not be so afraid. I could never admit it to these women who are so tough. I need to steal some of their strength.

The helicopter constantly hovering over the house isn't helping. From the attic it sounds like a machine gun.

The rest of the house is an oasis, though, quiet and peaceful. I've been hanging out with my roommates, and

Brix, and their friends. They're all very sincere and open, for punks. They're hippie punks, I guess—hippunks. They do instead of talk.

It's nice to have so many people around after so long of loneliness. Being with Sean, which was lonely in its own way, and then having him be away for work for such long stretches. After Ai left it was almost unbearable.

I've even been getting high with them sometimes. There's pot everywhere in this house. Brix's friend trades him stuff she grows for bike tune-ups. And Asha has a medical marijuana card—a green card, she calls it—and brings home all kinds of amazing edibles: truffles, caramel corn, smoothies, peanuts. The dispensary thing is new, I never imagined they'd have such fancy stuff. I was thinking maybe I should get a card, apparently it's easy. The pot calms me, most of the time.

That whole time in Japan, I never smoked with Sean when he had it. Maybe I was afraid of letting down my guard, relaxing into our life there, into him.

Now, I love how it helps me relax, similar to the Vicodin, but less numbed out. It's like I've been wound up like a spring my whole life, and someone's taken the two ends and pulled, made space for me to breathe.

I can get really spacey, though. Earlier I was looking everywhere for my phone—muttering to myself, "Great, I already lost my phone"—when finally I heard "Thanks for holding," and remembered that I was *on* my phone, waiting to make an appointment with the acupuncture clinic.

Sometimes after they get me high I find myself looking at the hippunks like an ape seeing humans for the first time, head cocked to the side, fascinated. Like a cultural anthropologist, able only to observe, not to engage.

I'm surrounded by women who are experimenting

with their lives, reworking the parts of themselves they don't want anymore. Lily and Asha told me about a former roommate of theirs who decided she wanted to be a guy. She had top surgery, the testosterone kicked in, she started passing—and then she changed her mind. She felt alienated and guilty, like she was turning her back on her womanhood. So now she's going back to being a woman.

I guess I get to change too. I'm getting a do-over, and I get to choose who I want to be this time.

I chose them, Lily and Asha—I could have lived anywhere in the world, with any kind of person, and I chose them.

January 17

3:47 a.m.

Just woke from a dream of Nara.

I knew it was Nara because I was surrounded by dozens of deer, in a huge open field. They were nuzzling me, and they tried to speak to me, in a language I didn't understand, no matter how hard I tried to decipher even one word of what they were saying. They started getting angry, butting me with their heads and nibbling at my clothes, repeating themselves louder and louder until I woke up.

That photo of the Nara Daibutsu in my guidebook, his hand beckoning me to come. I so wanted to go and offer him a prayer.

Now I look at the statue of the Nara Daibutsu that Yuki brought me from her trip there, sitting on my altar next to the Happy Home candle that finally burned out, the last of its flame dancing around the glitter and tiny silver stars at the bottom—and I think maybe he wasn't beckoning me to come, but warning me to stay away.

Now I am Nara. I think it suits me better than my birth name did. In Japan, of course, I could never have been so presumptuous. Though occasionally people did think I was Japanese, when my bangs covered my eyes.

My hair is getting long, to my shoulders, my bangs past my eyebrows. I miss Ryo. When he gave me this bob, he made it impossible for me to ever cut my own hair again. I could never do it like he did.

I miss my students. Their faces flood my head at night, their eyes confused. Oh, Kai-Kai. I miss you most.

I miss my friends. Clara and Yuki mostly. But also Ai. And Sean. The fact that I can't see them, that I might never see them again, makes my heart feel like a weight in my chest, like the rose quartz heart I gave Sean last Christmas. The one I left his note under.

Not nice, not nice at all. I was so out of my mind....

I imagine Clara striding through the streets of Tokyo with that butterfly on her back, neon flashing off its sequins. Yuki I see in my cozy black sweater with the big buttons, her hands deep in the pockets as she waits for the train.

January 18

I'm embarrassed to admit it, but when I hear the front door open two floors down, I listen for the heavy steps of Lily hoisting her bike up the long staircase. She takes her bike on BART and rides to UCSF, over the tracks and through the traffic of downtown S.F. and back. That's gotta be close to 10 miles round-trip, a lot of it uphill. Several times a week she does this.

Sometimes I go down to greet her. She'll smile weakly, if she's tired, as she sets her bike against the railing. But she always smiles.

I'm not the only one. Everyone loves Lily. She has a lot of friends, and they're over all the time. She plays her banjo and sings little ditties. I love to soak back into the green velvet couch and watch her. When she looks over, throws me a smile, none of my pain means a thing.

Brix joins in on the harmonica sometimes. He's such a sweet guy. Tall and bearded, with a light-brown mullet. But with Lily he's like a little boy. When they come back together after being away from each other, they touch, they look at each other, and that's all they need. All the answers in the eyes, in an instant.

Things grow for Lily. Once a week she puts all her plants in the clawfoot to water them, her own personal jungle.

I want to be around her all the time, and she's not around much, so there's always longing in me, for more time with her, more attention from her, always for more.

January 23

3:30 a.m.

Awake at 3:30 again. I take the valerian at night and it knocks me out, but in a few hours it fades and I pop awake.

In Japan when I had insomnia, the worry dolls Sean brought me from Guatemala were next to me, a tiny little family lined up on the molding next to my futon, in the corner where only I could see them. They helped me feel less alone when he was gone. I would actually tell them my worries, like they say you're supposed to, and sometimes I could get back to sleep then.

The little family is in the suitcase under my altar now, with the drawings from my students and all the other stuff I want to keep but not look at yet.

Now I just have Lily's white feather to calm me in the night. I rub it, close my eyes, concentrate on the softness.

The feather reminded me of my cashmere scarf, its softness against my neck on that scary night in Japan when I woke up all sweaty. So I got it and brought it into bed with me. Its sky blue is pretty against the red of Sadie's case, against the darker blood-red of the comforter.

I also took a Vicodin, to calm myself. There are only six left.

My defenses are down. They go down with the sun. Up here in the quiet all alone, it's just me and my fears.

Maybe it will help to type them out. Sadie can be my new worry doll.

<u>My Fears</u>

1. I'm crazy
2. Sean will find me

3. Sean will never forgive me
4. Lily and Asha will find out I've been lying
5. There's something wrong with me, some hole that can't be fixed
6. I won't be able to find a job and I'll run out of money
7. I'll always be afraid
8. I'll never fall in love again
9. I will fall in love again and I'll hurt them
10. Earthquakes

I think that's pretty much it. Not too bad, right Sadie? Ha ha.

Shit. I need help.

January 25

It's been raining for a week straight. We moved the backyard couch under the overhang of the house, and I'm sitting under here with Sadie now, looking out at the rain.

It reminds me of standing at the window of my apartment, or the window of the school, staring out through those tall panes of glass. When I think of Japan now that's what I see. Me looking for another world. For this world.

There I lived on the bottom of three floors, here I'm on the top. There it was sharp edges, shiny appliances… here it's all curvy lines, century-old oven. There it was bare, spare, white and silver, here every space is used, every room is a different color.

I didn't get to choose my place in Kamakura—it came with the job. Here, though what I was really choosing was Lily and Asha, I also knew a charming Victorian would be good for my soul. My eyes are soothed by its rounded edges. The smooth alive feel of the redwood railing grounds me as I climb the front stairs. The easy access to outside in the back helps me breathe, the kitchen door almost always open. Sometimes I come in the front door and walk straight through the house to the back porch.

I'm wearing my sky-blue raincoat, so glad I brought it with me. I was in the side yard earlier, admiring the house, when Ingy got home from school, only slightly surprised to find me standing in the rain outside her kitchen door. I love how non-judgmental she is. We walked all the way around the perimeter together, and she showed me the cut-outs edging the bottom of the roof, the curlicue gables at the corners, the fading pink and black and white paint job and where you can see the periwinkle underneath.

She loves how old and loony the house is, but it's just

normal for her. Claudia's lived here since Ingy was born—13 years. The landlord has been the same all that time, but Claudia and Ingy have seen lots of tenants in our space come and go. Other families like them, twentysomethings like us, even one older gentleman who lived here by himself for years…but Ingy told me Lily and Asha are her favorite.

She showed me her room, apologized for the mess, and it was impressively messy. It's a perfect square, in the back of the house, with the sound of the washing machine in the laundry room behind it and the smell of the roses outside her window. I thought of the white peaches outside my window when I was her age, how their sweet smell makes me nauseous now.

We hung out for a while. When I took off my raincoat, I was in my pajamas. I told her "I forgot to get dressed today," and she laughed. She played me some J-pop she'd just downloaded, and it was funny, the same songs that in Japan were irritating, in Ingy's room sounded cool. We sat on her bed and bobbed like buoys, and I thought, *They sound happy, not whiny. They've been happy all this time.*

January 29

Today Lily asked me if I'd seen her white feather. She said it's a dove feather, that Brix found it and gave it to her when they were first getting together.

I said no, I hadn't seen it.

I was nervous, though, and I looked over at Asha then and saw she was watching us. Maybe she's suspicious. Oh god, maybe they talked about this. Maybe this is their way of telling me to stay out of their rooms.

How embarrassing. I have to be more careful. It is so not worth getting caught.

January 31

1:11 a.m.
I was just startled awake by the house creaking with the wind. Sat up and hit my head on the eave. And then I thought I heard a baby crying.

Maybe I'm haunted. Fuck.

There's no way I can get back to sleep now. My head is throbbing, and I'm scared. Maybe someone's awake downstairs.

8:45 a.m.
I just came from Asha's bed. Her light was on when I went downstairs, so I whispered her name at her door. It sounded more like the wind—a breeze, then a hiss—than a name. But she heard me and opened the door and I told her I was scared and she let me in.

She was reading *Beloved,* and made space for me on the bed. She was wearing a furry black fleece with the hood on, the woman is always cold. Her glasses were on the bedside table, she doesn't need them for reading.

"I couldn't sleep." I wanted to tell her everything then. Instead I said, "The house is hella creaky up there."

"Yeah, it gets that way in the wind." She told me she has insomnia too, asked if she could make me something to help me sleep. I nodded, thankful, and sank back into her pillows, let them envelop me. The urge to tell her my secrets passed when she left the room. She seems to know everything anyway.

She came back and gave me a shot of lemon balm and some chamomile tea. Her chamomile was delicious, like none I'd ever tasted, and I wondered if she'd put a spell on it but did not ask. She got back under the covers and read to me as I drank my tea, a part of the ghost story that was sweet, not scary, about nature, and love. After a while I actually fell asleep. Her bed was so soft, like a cloud, I just floated away on it.

When I woke up, she was asleep. I very carefully got out of her bed, made myself tea and brought it back up here.

I think it's okay. Right, Sadie? To let myself be comforted? I can trust Asha, let her be there for me. That's why I came here. Right?

They said they would take care of me. In the ad. Right now that feels like all I want, in the whole wide world.

February 1

The rain finally stopped today, the sun took its place, and on cue the plum tree popped out its first blossoms. I swear, I'm not making this up.

Lily and I had a nice talk, looking out over the blossoming yard from the back porch. She was making cookies, vegan oatmeal cherry. I mixed up the dry ingredients for her.

We sat and shared a joint while they baked. She told me she wants kids, badly, but Brix doesn't. He knows how important it is to her. "But he says it's just not something he can do, no matter how much he loves me. He doesn't trust himself with a kid after the violence of his father."

I cried when she told me this. So embarrassing. She teared up a little too, even as she was laughing at me crying. Then we were both laughing at each other and crying at each other, sitting toe to toe, wiping our eyes with our sleeves and smiling. The sun was shining, and the neighbors' dogs were being quiet for once.

I told her I want a girlfriend. She said, "You shouldn't have trouble finding someone—you're so pretty."

I hope she didn't know I was thinking, *Too bad Brix got to you first.* Her Swedish mom and Jamaican dad created something truly special when they made her. She can look sweet and innocent like a child, and then in a second she's all sex, her amazing body tall and strong and curvy, undeniable. I've never been able to imagine being with a femme, until Lily.

But it's not essentially sexual, what I feel for her. Anyway, if anything ever did happen with her I'm sure I wouldn't know what to do, I'd probably just run away upstairs.

This is why I need more experience.
We made a list.

<u>What I'm Looking For</u>

1. cute
2. strong
3. sweet
4. stable
5. creative
6. connection (like plugging a three-prong into an outlet, that fit, that energy)

February 2

I'm sitting with Sadie out on the porch bench, in the sun. Eating some quiche from Sweet Adeline, the bakery at the corner. This morning, I must have stood staring at the pastries for a full minute, lost in rapture, paralyzed by my inability to choose just one. The people who work there must think I'm such a stoner.

I got a cookie for breakfast, and quiche for lunch. Eating a cookie for breakfast felt decadent, like something grown-ups do.

Having all that sweetness a block away makes up for the fact that I'm living next door to a crack house. Clara and Yuki would love it—how cliché can you fucking get? But they also would not be able to believe these pastries.

Most days it balances out, the good and the bad of this place. I like the people I live with. Brix tuned up a sweet brown Schwinn for me, so I can get around easily now. Stopped eating meat, which feels awesome. Don't think I can ever go vegan, or I'd have to give up the pastries.

It's weird not working. I've never not worked before. It makes me feel guilty sometimes, separate from the rest of the world. But I know it's temporary, and I know it's what I need. I worked my ass off in Japan. I deserve a little break.

Resting and recovering, that's my work now. And writing it all down.

February 3

I lost Sadie today. No one was home, and I spent a frantic hour like a chick in a horror flick, whipping around at all traces of red in the corner of my eye. I looked everywhere, even in Lily and Asha's rooms. I had told myself I wouldn't go in there anymore, but I was completely freaking out and starting to worry that one of them had read this.

I was terrified when I opened the door to Asha's room, sure I was going to see Sadie sitting ominously on her bed, bright red against the soft gray blanket.... I opened her door so slowly it creaked spookily. But Sadie wasn't there.

I was imagining their angry faces, what they would say to me if they learned my secrets. Not just the lies but all of my feelings for them, my fantasies, the feather…

Sadie was in my fucking bathroom. The last place I looked, the only place left to look. I did actually look in the downstairs bathroom, in the cupboards there, expecting to see Sadie sitting mischievously on the towels. Why would my fucking computer be in the downstairs bathroom cabinet? I was not making sense.

I was so freaked out, it got to the point where all I could think to do was write, and I came up here, but of course I couldn't write, because Sadie was gone. I went in my bathroom to pee finally and saw her sitting there on the floor, her red case perfectly centered on one of the black tiles.

I had taken her in there with me to poop this morning. I was in the middle of a very exciting Tetris game when I had to go. Got to level 12. Then I finished and set her down to wash my hands, and stonily went on to whatever else I was doing.

Oh, Sadie, I was so scared when I lost you! I was terrified that Lily or Asha had read this—but even more than that, I was worried I'd lost the journal. It's keeping me sane.

I password-protected the file, in case anyone ever does get curious. And tomorrow I'll go get one of those little sticks you can transfer files onto. That way if something ever does happen to Sadie, I won't have lost the journal too.

I kind of like it, my writing, sometimes. I can see how far I've come. This document is my proof.

February 4

I'm not a good person. I'm so ashamed of what I've done, I haven't even been able to think about it. Leaving Sean, hiding from him. Leaving the kids. What is wrong with me?

Being around Lily's light makes my darkness heavier when I leave her. I fall back into it, it falls back into me, I can't get out from under it.

I want to do the right thing. I want to make up for it somehow. But what is right, now? I have no idea.

I can't breathe when I think about what I did.

It's penance. Fuck breathing.

February 7

I threw away Lily's freaking sourdough starter, and she is not happy with me. I was making room for a bunch of stuff I'd gotten at the Berkeley Bowl, this amazing grocery store down the street. Lily let me take her station wagon there so I could stock up. It's like a farmer's market mixed with a grocery store mixed with a health food store. It feels like all of Berkeley is in there, navigating the narrow aisles, passively aggressive.

So I got home and needed to make space in the fridge, and the sourdough starter looked like moldy old food, so I threw it away.

Then Lily got home a little while ago, and just now she called up to the attic, "Nara, can you come down here?" When I looked down at her, even from the top of my stairs I could see that her eyes were on fire. I was a little afraid and I hurried down, slipping on the narrow attic stairs and hitting my ass hard, but hopping up like nothing happened and following her into the kitchen.

She flipped opened the lid of the trashcan and just stood there, looking at me.

She said, "What is that doing there?"

I rubbed my ass. I said, "Um, it's moldy food I threw away?"

She said, "That's my sourdough starter. I've been maintaining it since before you moved in." Like it was more important than me.

I said, "Oh, no."

She said, "Oh, yes."

I said, "I thought it was moldy food."

She said, "Why didn't you throw it in the compost, then? At least then I could have salvaged it." As it was it had other gross things stuck to it and it could definitely not be salvaged.

I felt terrible. And a little scared. There was nothing to say, so I just looked at her. She looked back at me like I was a very disappointing child. Shaking her head.

She said, "I have to start over now."

I said, "I'm sorry."

And she walked away from me, into her room, slammed the door. Now she's in there with the music turned up, and I came back upstairs. Bogus Basin, Brix's band, is pulsing under my feet.

They didn't know this before I moved in, but I am not one of their kind. I had no idea it's so hard to be a hippie. It's stressing me out. Claudia tried to explain the gray water system to me the other day. The used water from the washing machine is diverted to water the roses and the trees. But it's so complicated, I almost started crying as she was showing me. All I could do was nod, pretending to understand, worrying about fucking it all up.

In Japan, at least when I did something wrong I was usually blissfully unaware—they'd write notes in Japanese on my trash when I sorted it wrong, but I couldn't read the kanji. Of course I could have asked Haruka to read them to me, but the trash was already such a pain in the ass. Taking it out every day. Washing everything, sorting it, breaking it down… I was doing my best, and it was never enough.

It sucks, feeling that way here, with these people I want to be family with. Asha got pissed at me the other day for washing her cast iron pan with soap. I apologized, and she teased me, "Rookie move."

I want an easy house. I don't want to have to be trained on how to live. I don't want to have to feel afraid, every time I do something, that I'm doing it wrong.

I want to have ready-made food now and then, maybe even something processed. I don't want to have to eat what they eat, act like they act.

Already, being Nara is a struggle. Having to monitor everything I say, remember what I've said. If I'm tired, or emotional, or stoned, sometimes I just want to drop the charade and say fuck it.

And do what? That's where I get stuck.

This time is a weird bridge to something, but I don't know what yet. I'm like a hamster that's ventured into one of those tunnel mazes. I can't see what lies in which direction. All I can do is move forward blindly, either this way or that. Any minute now I'm going to step out onto a wheel, and I'll be spinning.

February 13

8:10 a.m.

Lily and Asha are fighting again. They woke me up. I got up and peed, then brought Sadie back into bed with me. Even though I put earplugs in, I can still hear the intensity flying around down there, the boom of their voices. Their anger echoes in me, it bounces around my body like I'm hollow.

It takes me back to those screaming matches with my mom, in high school. So weird to think about her again after all those years in Japan, feeling finally free of her. But being around all this female energy, and being geographically closer…I thought my parents would feel far away still, but SoCal feels dangerously close.

When she screamed at me, every part of me filled with hatred for her. I remember that feeling so clearly. But my hatred of her didn't protect me. She was still able to hurt me so badly. Why did she want to? She hated me too, I can see that now. But why? Because I stopped being a doll she could dress up and play with? I was learning who I was, and I didn't want her to have any say in that. It must have enraged her to have lost control of me—she pulled way back on the reins. She was trying to break me.

And now I'm afraid if I go downstairs, Lily or Asha could lash out and hurt me like my mom did. Because when a person reaches that point they are capable of terrible things. Like an animal.

They're fighting about Lily waking Asha up this morning. L likes to be in the kitchen before she leaves for school in the morning, cleaning and cooking. But A's bed is right on the other side of the kitchen, so inevitably she gets woken up, much earlier than she wants. Her schedule is more flexible than L's, and she sets it up so she can sleep late, but then L comes in and wakes her up. Lily is a morning person, and Asha is a night person—apparently it's been an issue for years.

So this morning, Asha banged hard on the wall of the kitchen, which must have knocked something off the kitchen shelf. I woke up to a crash.

Lily was pissed. I heard her scream, "Come in here and clean this shit up!"

They get to fury fast. There's so much they've compromised over their three years together in this house, they forget their love and respect for each other and it's just raw emotion raging. I don't know how they come back from that. I remember Clara and Yuki, how beautifully they always got along. Of course I wasn't always there, but I can't even imagine them having a blowout like this one.

Brix explained some of this to me, about Lily and Asha's dynamic, the last time they got into a fight, a few days ago. He was here, and when they started in on each other—that time in Lily's room about bills—he and I retreated to the back porch. I told him it freaked me out, seeing Lily especially like that. "Me too, at first," he said. "I call her Tiger Lily when she's like that."

"I met her the other day, Tiger Lily. When I threw away her sourdough starter."

"Oh yeah, she told me about that. She felt terrible."

That felt good to hear. "It was nothing like this though."

"Yeah, she only really gets to that fever pitch with Asha."

Brix told me L and A both come from hot-headed families, where yelling was how they communicated. So they let it all out, and then usually the energy just dissipates.

"My dad was a dictator," he said. "He ruled with his belt." He has such a lovely face, and usually, when Lily's around, it's full of her light. But now that I'm getting to know him better, I can see that it's holding a lot. When he started talking about this shit, he aged twenty years in a second. And at the same time, I could see the scared little boy, battling his father. The unfairness of it etched in his skin.

"Did you ever fight back?" I asked him. I don't know why I asked, I guess I was feeling close to him, and I wanted to know.

"No. I just got smarter over the years, learned how to avoid him."

I nodded. "In my family, my mom told us what to do, and my dad and I did it. And if we didn't…she never hit me, but she could be scary."

Brix's mom divorced his dad when he was in high school, and he moved out with her, into her small apartment. His sister had moved in with friends, so it was just Brix and his mom, and for a year they had a glimpse of the happy life they could have had. Then he graduated and moved into his friend Merry's garage, the one he's in the band with, and lives with. They were making music even back then. He told me he would sometimes roll right out of bed onto his drum kit.

"I'd just start playing, before I even went to pee, man. And they were cool with it. Merry's mom was so cool. I never had a drum set at home, obviously, I would just always practice at Merry's. I got really good after I moved there."

He's still tight with Merry's mom, and over the years he's gotten to be close with his own mom too—he chose to forgive her for not protecting him. His sister lives in Boise still, where they grew up. She's married, with a kid, and Brix sees them a lot, they come and stay with him at his house in East Oakland. He said I should come over to their house one of these days, meet the chickens, and Merry. They make music in their own garage now.

His dad lives alone, in the same country house outside Boise. Brix hasn't seen him since he left, and he says he never will.

We were both so shaken by the fight happening in the other room, we didn't have any energy for anger in that moment. But now when I think about what he told me, I think, *Fuck that. That man should be punished.* No one has the right to harm another human being, and harming someone you love is unforgivable.

That's why the fighting is so hard to take. Because they are just hurting each other down there. And we have all had enough hurt for this lifetime, enough damage has been done. It's too terrible to hurt each other more. I don't care if that makes me too passive, like Asha says. I can't take it.

I imagine them like cats tussling down there, Tiger Lily leaping and growling, Asha fierce and fast as a panther.

February 14

I made veggie sushi for Asha and Lily tonight. The tension in the house after their fight really sucked, so I thought, *Sushi.*

And it's Chinese New Year. I refuse to acknowledge the Hallmark holiday happening today, but I was excited to celebrate the Lunar New Year, after my years in Japan, where they don't. And…we celebrated with sushi and sake. We rolled the sushi on our plates, I showed them how.

Most of the fillings came from our CSA box.

<u>Oaktown Sushi Fillings</u>

1. carrots
2. cucumbers
3. asparagus, roasted, w/ olive oil and lemon
4. avocado
5. sautéed chard w/ garlic
6. shiitake mushrooms, braised in tamari
7. mashed yam with sesame
8. *tamago,* from Brix's chickens

My favorite combo was avocado/chard/shiitake. Lily kept making gang signs and saying, "Yo, that's how I roll."

We'd eat for a while, then take a break to have a smoke or dance around to this awesome Bollywood music Lily put on. Then we'd make more sushi.

I got one of my favorite brands of sake at the Berkeley Bowl—they have a good selection. I told them how in Japan you never fill your own glass, and we all started filling one another's glass and I lost track. I always did love the sake high the best.

They've moved on from their fight finally, but there's an almost competitive vibe between them now. I'm dying to know if anything has ever happened between them. Lily was being super affectionate with me, and Asha seemed jealous, of who I have no idea. I couldn't tell if Lily was flirting with me, or fucking with Asha, or if she was just happy and drunk.

It felt so good, Lily's arm around me. My body warmed where she touched it.

Asha just shook her head, watching Lily, and said, "You are such a Leo."

They teased me about looking for a girlfriend. Asha and I made a plan to go to the gay bar up the street soon.

We ate for hours. Every time I'd start to clear the table they'd stop me, saying since I cooked they should clean, and anyway they weren't done eating.

I kept singing "It's the Year of the Tiger," to the tune of "The Eye of the Tiger."

The Year of the Tiger Lily.

February 18

I was in the kitchen making tofu burgers tonight and Asha came home from helping her friend have a baby. She had blood on her jeans, which she showed me casually then proceeded to tell me all about the birth. As I mixed the crumbled tofu with the bread crumbs and onions, my hands all slimy, I couldn't stop thinking about how slimy Asha's hands must have been when she held the baby after it was born, and suddenly all the blood rushed to my head and I felt like I was going to pass out, or throw up, or both.

My ears were ringing, I couldn't hear anything. I ran to the bathroom and lay down on the cool floor until it passed.

I came back out to Asha asking if I was okay. I nodded weakly, but she could see that I was scared. She took me out to the porch, then went back in and changed out of her bloody jeans and into yoga pants. She gave me a shot of milk thistle leaf, then pulled some rose oil out of her pocket and massaged my hands. I thought, *Well, if she is a witch she's a good witch.* I started to cry a little, I couldn't help it, it felt so good to be cared for.

She didn't ask any questions. I guess she knew I didn't want to talk. Or maybe she knew what was wrong. Maybe I'm totally transparent, despite my ridiculous efforts to hide what's happened. Clearly I can't hide it from myself anymore. I need to start dealing.

When she could see I was better, she lit an American Spirit. We smoked, then we went back into the kitchen, and she got the tomato, pickles, lettuce ready while I fried up the burgers. Then we called Lily to join us and she took a break from her studying and we ate and played Scrabble like a little family. Asha kicked our asses, of course.

February 19

I started bleeding again today. I had terrible cramps, so I took a Vicodin, then tried to soak the rest of the pain away in the bath.

I've been taking a bath in the clawfoot almost every day since I got here. I try to bathe when Asha and Lily are out, so I'm not hogging their bathroom.

The best moment of my day is when my body sinks into the water. It's a great fucking tub, plenty long enough for me to stretch out. I like to lie flat on my back, my head underwater. It feels so good to be submerged. It's my meditation, everything quiet and clear. Like the Vicodin felt in those early days.

Today Asha walked in on me. The light was off, with just a candle burning, so she thought the bathroom was empty when she came home. She opened the door and was sitting down on the toilet when I said "Hi."

I startled her. Her big brown eyes, the candle catching the lift of her lashes, looked at me like I was Gollum. Maybe it was my quiet, my calm. I didn't mind her seeing me naked, didn't bother to cover myself.

Her eyes were so big without her glasses, which were sticking out of the pocket of her denim shirt. She finished peeing and was outta there.

I have no idea what goes on in that brainy Indian head. The one thing I know for sure is that it never stops.

February 24

Today we made three quiches from scratch. Lily and Ingy rolled out the crust on our Formica table. Ingy put on some dub, so loud and with so much bass, it felt like it was coming from inside me. It was impossible not to move to it. Every now and then Ingy broke out in a head-banging grooving that was surprisingly self-assured for a preteen. She's so different from me at her age. Like I wish I'd been.

I asked Asha what I could do to help. She looked at me, her glasses fallen down her nose, hands too busy chopping veggies to adjust them. I gently pushed them up, and she smiled, disarmed. It was a sweet sight to see. She's really quite beautiful, no matter how hard she tries to hide it.

"What about cheese?" I said, smiling back at her. We were stoned, and enjoying some wine Lily had been saving for a special occasion, which she decided was today. Ingy was having some too.

"Non, non, mon cheri. Ze fromage ees no vegan." Cooking brings out Asha's French side.

"Si, por supuesto," I said. I've been practicing my Spanish with Claudia. "Pero…los huevos?"

"Brix's chickens are happy, so it's okay," Lily called over as she and Ingy cut three circles in their table of dough with a pot lid.

"You wanna whip?" Asha asked me.

"Oh, yeah, baby," I replied.

The tension between us, I've chalked up to just two lonely new lesbians considering whether it's a good idea to hook up. I'm still pretty sure it's not a good idea, though I'm getting hornier by the day, which makes it hard. Ha ha. We went out a few nights ago to a benefit at El Rio, my first time into S.F. since I've been back. I was slightly paranoid at first that I'd see Dani, or one of Sean's friends, but then I had a few drinks and forgot to care. Asha drank too much and vomited in the bathroom, then held my hand on the BART ride home. We took a cab home from Ashby, I put her to bed when we got home, and we haven't mentioned it since.

Now she was circling the whisk above her head and gyrating her hips. *Maybe we should just get it on and get it over with.*

But Asha hasn't been with a woman yet and I do not want to be her teacher. On the other hand, some harmless fun could be…harmless. And fun.

As I whipped the eggs. I thought, *I am high on estrogen. This is what I've been missing all these years, what I've been needing.* Lily said when she went to retrieve the eggs from Brix's hutch today, there were an even dozen.

Lily and Ingy lay their three circles into their tins. Lily was so good with Ingy, showing her how but then trusting her to do it herself, okay with it not being perfect.

I tried all of the quiches—carrot/mushroom, garlic/potato, and avocado/leek. Almost as good as Sweet Adeline's.

February 27

Another big earthquake today, off the coast of Chile. It was an 8.8, the sixth largest earthquake ever recorded by a seismograph. Triggered a tsunami, which reached all the way to Japan. Hundreds dead and lost, homeless.

I've been obsessively reading about it, carrying Sadie up and downstairs with me. As if I can do anything about it. As if knowing makes a difference.

March 4

I saw Bogus Basin perform tonight! Lily couldn't come, she had to study, so Asha and I went, to this Berkeley bar called the Starry Plough. It's old and rickety like a saloon, but with hippies instead of cowboys.

They're really good, very funky. Brix plays the drums and harmonica and sings. He's an awesome drummer and looked so beautiful up there, glowing like a hippunk Jesus, with this deep, matter-of-fact voice that reminds me of Bill Callahan.

Merry has a really strong voice too, and she's an incredible guitar player. They've been playing together for so long, their songs sort of hang off of them casually, effortlessly. They definitely rock out, but on some slower folk songs Merry sat down on an amp and finger-picked, relaxed. Some of their songs are goofy, making fun of high school drama or politics, but they also go deeper. Merry sang a song about unrequited love that was really sweet and sad, and Brix sang a song that I think was about his dad, about writing him off.

I learned tonight that this is how her name is spelled, Merry, so I search-and-replaced it in the earlier entries. Brix told me, after the show while she was talking to some fans, that her mom came up with her name on the spot when she was born, because she hadn't cried a peep, and just seemed really happy to be there. Also, her mom loves *The Lord of the Rings.* She bought two sets of the books for Brix and Merry when they were 12, and they read the books together.

They reminded me of the familiarity that Sean and I had, when you've known someone for so long you know what they'll do next. I didn't realize I missed it, having Sean as my friend. I wish we'd never tried to be anything more.

I studied Merry's hands on her guitar, admired Brix's efficiency on the drums, watched him whisper into his harmonica, his eyes seeking Merry's.

I wanted to know what they were saying to each other. Lily and Brix have it too—their own language.

Merry is so sweet, very earthy and accessible, with curly brown hair that's shaved on one side and growing out fuzzy. A huge smile, and giant blue eyes. And so talented.

Asha got annoyed by my fawning. She's seen them perform a bunch of times already, and shows of enthusiasm seem to make her uncomfortable. Plus I had decided that I really should not risk complicating things in the house with Asha—maybe she felt me backing off and didn't like it.

Riding our bikes home she went extra fast, like she was racing me. Finally I just gave up and let her go. It was quiet out and I wanted to enjoy it. When I got home she was sitting waiting for me at the top of the steps. She said, "Slowpoke," and went in the bathroom.

I officially have a crush on Merry now. I'd give anything to be able to do what she does, to hold people captive like that.

March 6

Today Asha and I hung out in her room, and I kept having the urge to hold her hand again. I am really wanting that contact, I don't know if it's even romantic. I think maybe it's like in India how little boys, and even grown men, hold hands walking down the street. She said she grew up with that, it's comfortable for her, and maybe that makes it feel comfortable for me too.

But I'm too afraid to give her the wrong idea. I'm not sure what I want from her, with her. I've been fantasizing about her when I masturbate, so now I can't help thinking of her in a sexual way when we're together. I wish we could have sex in a parallel universe, then come back to our sweet home and just be building our friendship like before. I'm afraid to mess this up. Because when it comes down to it, the house is the priority. It's the net I'm knitting for myself.

Plus, Asha seems determined to be miserable. Maybe she thinks it's who she is. Death, famine, patriarchy define her. Or maybe they're her protection, from having to feel anything personal, private.

She has darkness in her past, implied that she had a boyfriend who was abusive. It made her tougher, politicized her. After all the disappointments men have handed down over the years, Asha decided, fuck 'em. But as sure as she is that she wants to be with a woman, she seems terrified of actually doing it. She'd rather just hear my stories. She asked if I was with any women in Japan.

So I told her the story of Ai. Which means "love" in Japanese. "I answered her ad seeking a language partner. I wasn't even looking for anything more."

Asha nodded at me, like, *Yeah, right.*

"I wasn't! The culture is so conservative, I had given up

on finding a woman." Plus I had a boyfriend. "But when I saw Ai I was blown away. She had amazing style. Just completely unique. She was the only Japanese woman I knew who took risks like that. She had traveled a ton, to more than 50 countries. So she had all these incredible clothes from all over, and she never wore the same thing twice.

"She had a worldliness and was ten years older than me, which was kind of hot. She liked knowing more than I did.

"We started meeting in a café every Friday afternoon, to practice her English, which was perfect, and my Japanese, which was a mess. We had so much fun together. Our language practice turned into bitchfests and therapy sessions. We'd usually end up spending hours chatting, first in Japanese, but eventually ending up in English.

"Our Friday afternoons stretched into Friday night dinners. She showed me her favorite pubs in Kamakura."

We went a lot at this bar by the train station. She opened up to me there, told me things she'd never told anyone. The old wood in there had felt like it could absorb anything you handed it. As I watched her speak those unspeakable things, I wanted to hold her, kiss it away.

Thinking about it now, knowing what I knew about her leveled our power dynamic. It softened her and made her feel more accessible, and it made me more confident. I knew that I wanted more, and I knew that she wanted more, whether or not she would have admitted it. Finally something I knew more about than she did. My time with Dani may have been short, but I learned a lot.

"A few times we took the train to Tokyo. Or we would cook at my house." When Sean was away. He knew about Ai—he knew enough, from how I talked about her not to ask for details.

"She taught me how to make perfect ramen. But she always went home at the end of the night. The end just got further and further away from the beginning."

Asha and I went out to the porch to smoke a joint. She was quiet, subdued.

"Ai had never been with a woman—it was my move to make. And so late one night, last summer, we were walking home—there are these amazing hidden walking paths in Kamakura, with no cars, and one of them went straight from the bar to her house. We were both wearing dresses, and it felt so good, the warm air on our skin, being alive and drunk and outside in the night. Just before we rounded the corner to her place, I stopped and kissed her."

Asha's eyes got big, and she let out a big lungful of smoke. "Shit! What happened?"

"It was not a skillful kiss. It was awkward, and she pulled away immediately. It wasn't smart of me to wait until we were so close to her house, where her husband was probably waiting up for her."

I looked at Asha to see whether she'd get judgy. The pot was making me feel floaty. I thought I saw some anger or something in her eyes, behind her glasses, but she just said, "Go on."

"There's not much else to tell. She pulled away and said, in her perfect English, 'I have a husband. I am not gay.' And that was the last time I saw her. I emailed her an apology the next day, but she never wrote me back, and I was too humiliated to try again."

"Wow. Harsh."

"Yeah. It sucked."

That image of Ai, just after she pulled away from me. She comes into my head sometimes, and it's always that image, the last one I have of her. In her red dress, backing away from me, the memory of red on her lips, from her lipstick or mine. Did she know that was the last time she would see me? I could have sworn I saw longing in her eyes.

And then she turns away. Her hair in a knot on top of her head, one piece floating down her smooth white back as she walks away from me.

March 18

I wish I was the kind of person who just acted without thinking too much. Like when I came here, I made the decision quickly, I just knew what to do and I did it. But then, I didn't really have a choice—my intuition was all that was working.

I wonder if Sean's still living in Japan. It feels so far away now, so foreign. Sometimes it's hard to believe that was me there with him.

This house has become my world. Its smells are my smells. I move with its rhythms. Maybe now I don't know how to move on my own anymore. Less and less, I'm the puppet master in the attic…the more time I spend down here with them, the more they are moving me.

I want the comfort of her hand in mine. I look at it and my desire for this is almost unbearable. But I know from there I'd want more, I'd want her hand all over me, inside of me…and that could destroy everything. Nara can't make those kinds of mistakes.

So I suppress my urges. I try not to stare at her beautiful hands as she pulls tarot cards for me. The Empress, first, representing me. The card shows her calmly gazing into the future, holding a shield adorned with the symbol of Venus, planet of love.

Death, crossing her. Asha said not to be afraid, since this card can represent rebirth. Death rides a white horse and carries a flag bearing the mystic rose, symbol of life.

The Queen of Cups, my destiny. She's coming, Asha said, and she will be sensitive, passionate, sensual. Both of us wondering if she's Asha, or some other queen.

The Ten of Wands, referring to my recent past, representing struggle, strife, being stuck. No surprise there. The guy on the card wearily carries ten long flowering stalks. My heart hurt, seeing it. He's all alone, in the dark.

I need to get out of this house. I need to scream, to come. I need another pair of hands to obsess over.

Queen of Cups, come and fucking get me. I'm ready.

March 19

I woke up early again this morning, from a nightmare in the bamboo forest at Hokokuji Temple. I was winding around the narrow stalks like a pinball, following someone. Whoever it was kept slipping in and out of my vision. I needed to know who it was, but I couldn't go any faster.

I looked up, and glittering down through the tops of the tall green stalks I saw entities, spirits, dozens of them, darting and hovering. They were vague, almost translucent, would have been invisible if not for the sun's light.

Suddenly I was the one being chased. I didn't know who was behind me either, but now I was afraid to find out and tried to run. Again, I could barely move, the bamboo was so thick around me.

I hit my head on the ceiling again when I woke, and then started crying and couldn't stop, that feeling of being chased still in my bones....

Who was I following? Were they then following me?

Whoever it was, they're getting close.

I couldn't get back to sleep, and I was so spooked, and so sick of everything—super claustrophobic, stuck in the house, trapped in this stupid new life. I felt like I was going to explode if I stayed inside one more second. I pulled on a bra under my sleep clothes and took off running.

I let my body take over. I've never run in my life, not like that, but after a while the rhythm of my Sauconys on the pavement calmed me down and I started to feel a satisfaction in this new power—which I need, which is coming just at the right time.

I can get away if I need to. It turns out I have stamina. I felt like I could outrun anyone, like no one could catch me.

I ran over the train tracks and under the Highway 80 overpass, until I was stopped by the bay. I clambered down over the rocks and leaned over.

And then it all came out. Lava boiled up from inside me and out into the dirty water.

When I looked up from vomiting, there was San Francisco. I shivered as I saw it sitting there, as humbly glorious as always. So close, so patient. I sat down on the rocks and looked out at the skyline, gulped the bay air.

Then, in the dark dawn light, with no money on me, no water, no defenses—the images came. Everything I've been blocking. The kids, all of their pale, terrified faces. All that blood, blackening the rainbow rug. Thinking of it made me retch again, but nothing came out this time.

I'd done such a good job of pretending it never happened, I never lost her, I never even had her to lose, that I had forgotten. I was scared when I realized, scared of the damage I could do here.

If I am dissociating, where do I go and what do I do while I'm gone? If I'm not, on whose authority was I acting when I erased my memories of the events of January 6? I wasn't writing everything down yet then, I don't have a document of those hours, or contact with anyone who knows. And maybe it's just my system protecting me, but now it seems like what really happened may be much different from what I had constructed for myself to remember.

I sat for hours, watching the clouds lift their veil from the city, watching it start to sparkle in the sun. I thought of the jobs I had there and the apartments I lived in, and that started to feel like a third me. Maybe I've gone insane, to have split so thoroughly, so deeply. How can you ever really know for sure?

The cars and trucks rushing by to the Bay Bridge made

it look easy. S.F. has felt so far away, but it's just right there. Which means that my fear of seeing someone I know, and Sean or others finding out where I am, is real. Only a bridge and some water away.

I blinked heavily, again and again, against remembering. *The world will pause when I close my eyes. I don't have to open them until I'm ready. Then the world will play again.* But when I closed my eyes, the tortured eyes of my students floated in my head, their hands reaching for me. A terrible choked cry escaped me, as I remembered how much I loved them. How much they'd loved me. What they'd witnessed, which must have broken their hearts. I would have been the only one to heal that hurt, but I had left them with it.

Luckily I was all alone down there on the rocks, no one to wonder about the weird girl in her jammies making strange sounds and vomiting.

The kids were what had gotten me through the hard times. I see that now. They understood how to be comforting. They didn't let me get too quiet. They asked gentle favors of me. It's coming back to me—the sensation of comfort, that warm and satisfying loved feeling. All those eyes, so bright, all those smiles, adoring me. I haven't even let myself miss them. Because what can I do with it? Teaching isn't an option anymore. Not after that, no fucking way.

I imagine traveling back to Kamakura by boat, under cover of night. Past Alcatraz, under the Golden Gate Bridge, all the way through the Pacific to Yuigahama beach, where my seahorse sleeps. Beach of summer nights, of sparklers, of jellyfish that stung everyone but me. It's a perfect arrow from here to there.

How will I ever integrate my now with my then? All

that happened there, and all that's here now. There's no bridge.

I was as close, down on those rocks, as I'll ever get.

SPRING

March 21

There's a story about a man from Nagoya who killed himself in the spring, because he couldn't stand the sound of the word. Like Nina Simone sang, "I should never think of spring, for that would surely break my heart in two."

Cherry blossoms. In my head, they cover everything, like a virus.

I remember hiding inside the big, blooming cherry tree at the elementary school, looking out at the kids from behind the blossoms.

I had a small class that day, the last day before spring break, so Haruka let me take them for a walk on my own. We wound through the walking path like a caterpillar, and when we got to the elementary school the giant sakura tree stopped me in my tracks, train cars bumping into one another behind me. I'd never seen it in bloom.

I walked away from them then and they watched as I circled around the tree admiringly, then ducked inside, peering out at them. They giggled. They definitely thought I was weird.

In the empty space between trunk and branches, as I gazed out at the pink-dotted sky, I remember thinking, *This is why I came here.* I was lured by an idea of Japan as a place of uncorrupted nature. Though the truth was more complex, that sense of wonder made me more inclined to step inside a tree—something I probably wouldn't have thought to do at home.

I leaned back, felt the roots at my feet and the bark at my back. I resisted the urge to invite my students in, instead watched them wander off to explore on their own. I grabbed onto a branch on either side of me, held tight as my body vibrated with gratitude.

That moment was almost worth all the hard stuff that happened after.

I had wanted to climb into the tree and spend the day there. Instead I went back out into the real world and found my students, blew bubbles for them to chase and pop. Then they blew bubbles, and I attacked them with kung fu moves, chopping and kicking, no bubble left behind.

That tree is probably blossoming now. The tree in front of the building where I lived and taught probably is too. The whole country is blossoming, without me. Is Sean there with them?

Or is he here, nearby somewhere, looking for me? I thought that not-knowing, not being in touch with him, would protect me somehow, but it's making me vulnerable too. He could be anywhere.

Sean always did love a jump-scare. Sometimes when I leave the house, I worry he's waiting just outside the front gate, for me to emerge.

March 22

4:44 a.m.

Up again in the middle of the night again. Two of my cracked-out neighbors got in a fight and woke me, and now I can't get back to sleep. Maybe I should take a Vicodin. Only three left, I'm saving them for emergencies. Is this an emergency? The stakes feel high, in the dark.

Anxiety is so cliché, I keep trying to reject it as no more than a symptom of the world around me. *All this anxiety is giving me anxiety!* But there's no other word for this full-bodied fear.

Ever since the bamboo dream, I can't shake the feeling that something is coming for me. I wanted to be as not a part of the world as possible. After all those years being judged by my students and their parents, all my neighbors gossiping about the weirdo foreigner, I just wanted a quiet, private life. But it's not safe out there. I don't feel safe here.

My box of Japan stuff arrived from Clara. Seeing it, the way I packed everything, brought back that terrible time when I left. I was crazy.

I wish now I hadn't asked her to send it. A box of things I don't need, for what? So I can torment myself? I didn't open it, just put it under my altar with all the other stuff I'm avoiding.

Sleep, sleep, back to sleep. Wish Sadie had a lullaby for me. Or a story. This journal is the only one she has, and it's no bedtime story.

March 23

I'm reading *The Wind-Up Bird Chronicle* finally. In it the main character goes down into a well for long periods of time, days on end in darkness with no food. He starts to lose himself after a while, his body and then his mind, and once he's free of them all sorts of other interesting things start to happen.

I totally identify with this guy. I feel like that up here—like the attic is my well. I've closed the windows and the curtains, locked the door, am independent of the world. Not checking my phone or email, and definitely not my new Facebook account.

Fully detached and self-sufficient. I brought PBJ stuff up here, and I bought an electric kettle, so I can make tea and Cup O' Noodles.

I have two Vicodin left. I took one today, and it was just what I needed.

I'm not someone who needs people. I can stay up here as long as I want, I can stay up here forever, where it's safe and warm and quiet and clear.

Free of obligation, expectation. I'm free. Finally.

March 25

I'm trying to find the humor in my situation. I spend four years trapped in a relationship, a contract, a country, only to escape and then trap myself in an attic. Ha. Ha.

I haven't left the attic in four days. I don't want to deal with my roommates, don't have the energy to try and explain anything, it's just simpler to stay up here. Just taking some sick days.

Asha banged on the locked door for a while last night, called up, "Nara? What is going on up there?"

I yelled down, "I'm sick! Don't want to get you sick too. I'll be down soon."

I could practically hear her processing this. I sat stone-still, waited to see what she'd do. Finally she said, "Do you need anything?" I yelled down that I'm good, and then I heard her walk away.

I can't let them find out who I really am. I don't want to be Sara who miscarried, then fled. Sara who was in a relationship with a guy for four years because it was easy.

So I sit still, I try not to make any sound. In my shell. In the quiet of my well. I need to stay in this stillness a little longer.

Wearing Ai's Depeche Mode shirt, which smells like it's so ripe it's rotting. It was in the box of stuff Clara sent and I put it on and haven't taken it off. It feels good to get dirty, to let things fall apart.

I'm having a weird Japan nostalgia-fest up here. Clara had stuffed a bunch of snacks in the box too and they couldn't have come at a better time. It's like now that I'm scared of being found, this place is sullied, and I want what I had there instead. But I can't go back. I've exiled myself.

I've been thinking a lot about Ai. She was just one

more thing I packaged up and put away when I left. Ai, who broke my heart just a few months ago. I couldn't deal, so I got pregnant and forgot her.

But now I can't stop remembering. We were so close. In some ways I was closer to her than I've ever been to anyone. The way we trusted each other.

It was terrible, losing her, losing our Fridays together, which were what got me through my week. It was the beginning of the end of Japan, for me.

All I could do was bundle her secrets along with mine, inside me. And this T- shirt, from her first concert, back in the '80s, when I was just a toddler. She left it at my place, and I considered returning it to her, but I couldn't bear to lose it. And now I'm so glad I kept it, it's a silly thing but it's so soft, it's given me so much comfort. It reminds me of the feeling of safety I had with her, the ease we had together.

I think she was afraid of our ease, of how easy I made it to turn over the secrets she'd guarded all her life. It made her feel like a traitor, especially since I was a gaijin, not to be trusted. Not like that.

After Ai left me I leaned into Sean, my old home, told him I was ready to try and get pregnant, thinking it would take years. And then a month later I was pregnant, and I fell into it fully, the perfect distraction. I never saw Ai again, though for those last few months I was always afraid of running into her at the fancy grocery store, or rounding the corner on my bike and crashing into her. A part of me wanted that, of course, wanted to see her again, see what her eyes could tell me.

Then I lost Willow. I think now that if I'd had Ai to help me through that, maybe I could have stayed. I actually thought of calling her that night when I got home from the hospital, that desperate night before I started this journal. I was all alone, and I had this feeling that she was the only one who could help me. Maybe she could have, if I'd been brave enough to call her. But I called Clara instead.

I had been so sure that Ai wanted me too. But either I'd been wrong, or she'd been too afraid. Why are the women I love so afraid to love me back? I had rationalized that I was in a relationship too, and it never would have worked. Though deep down I knew that Sean would have been okay with it, or at least would have understood. I was dreaming of being with a woman again the whole time we were together—literally, all of the sex dreams I had when I was with him were about women. He knew that. He knew what I was giving up to be with him. So he would understand if I needed to explore that part of myself. Or so I told myself. We would deal with it, just like we'd dealt with everything.

The feeling that there wasn't anything we couldn't handle, together—it should have made me less inclined to want to cheat on him. But it didn't. It was what allowed me to be with him. And to leave him.

But I may have broken us for good when I left.

March 26

Today I did my first real butoh, outside my head. I moved my body this time. It felt good to let it do what it wanted. To crawl into the fire.

I was naked, had finally taken a shower and wasn't ready to get dressed. It's warm up here and dark like a cave, with just a few candles burning.

I was sitting on my bed and listening to Jeff Buckley's "Hallelujah" on repeat. I needed something to break me down, to make me feel something other than the same dull fear. On like the fifth or sixth listen I heard his sigh at the beginning and I crawled out of bed, fists first like an orangutan. I started tossing my wet hair around, side to side, on my hands and knees. I arched my back up like a hissing cat and then let it sink down, down, down, arms stretched out in front of me, hands pressing into the carpet. Child's pose.

The last time I did child's pose I was covered in blood. I remembered how it felt so clearly, I could feel the blackness pouring out of me again, my hands stuck to the rainbow.

Up here in the attic, I pushed myself away from the carpet, back onto my feet as though to stand, but my butt fell down into a squat. My hands grabbed on to the opposite knees, pushed down, raising my bare ass into the air, then letting it drop, again and again. My hair swinging forward and back, my hands pushed back, back, on my legs until they locked in place. I was perfectly halved, doubled in upon myself.

My hands pushed down on my neck, until my head was between my ankles, something I could not normally do. My hands told my body what to do and it listened.

I opened my eyes and looked out at the upside-down

world. Then my hands reached around my ankles and covered my eyes.

Jeff Buckley continued to sing and it broke me like it does every time. I fell over and curled into a ball, curled up small.

Then I fought my urge to hide, to die, and stretched my body out, arms overhead, back arched, toes pointed…but then falling back in and holding myself tight against the pain, head curled in like a roly-poly.

All I wanted was to stay curled up, safe within myself. But ever-so-slowly, I started to uncurl my body again. As slowly as a fern unfurling.

It was only because of the dark suspense of what I would find when I opened up, opened my eyes, that I was able to do it.

March 27

Asha knocked again earlier and I finally let her in. I didn't have the energy to fight back anymore. She came up here and looked around the room, at the dishes stacked on the windowsill, at me sitting on my bed with my computer and clothes and books all around me. She sat down at my desk chair, scrunched her nose at the smell.

"Are you feeling better?" she asked, overly sweet.

"A little," I said. "I think I had some kind of stomach virus."

"Mm-hmm. Nara, I don't know why you can't just tell me the truth."

"What do you mean? I seriously was sick."

"For five days? You don't leave your room for five days? What have you been eating?" She looked again at the dishes.

"I haven't been hungry," I said quietly.

"What happened to your hair?" she asked.

"Oh, I stopped blowdrying it. Turns out it's curly."

"What? You never knew you had curly hair?" She laughed and I did too. "That's funny. Really?"

"Yeah. I have a lot more time in my day now."

She laughed for a while then. She looked relieved. But she wasn't gonna let me off the hook that easy.

"Nara, I care about you, you know. It's not cool to just disappear on someone when they care about you. I was worried."

"I know, dude. I'm sorry. I just needed some time alone."

"Please don't call me dude. And next time, will you please just communicate with me? Text me, at least. I can help you, if you need it."

"Okay. I'm sorry. You're right. I won't do it again."

"Good. Now, want to go to the White Horse with me?"

And then it was my turn to laugh. I knew how badly she wanted me to say yes, to make everything okay again, but I was not ready to go downstairs, much less out, much less to a gay bar.

She narrowed her eyes, trying to figure out what the hell is wrong with me. Just a few weeks ago I was confiding all of my sad-girl tales, and now I am not telling her anything. She doesn't know what else to do, so she's trying to coax me out of the house—the sure cure for depression.

I feel terrible about my lies and afraid they will find out and hate me. Luckily Lily has been busy with school and at Brix's a lot. But Asha…I don't deserve her compassion, I can't accept it. And I can't tell her why I can't leave the house. I can't talk about the baby, or Sean. If I start, it's all gonna come flooding out, and there will be drama, and I can't handle any of that right now.

While she was up here I was just squirming inside, waiting for her to leave. The way she looks at me actually hurts, like she's trying to see into my soul, when all I want is not to be seen at all. She finally got the hint and left me to it, actually shaking her head as she went down the stairs.

I set this trap, and then I walked right into it.

March 29

Claudia has been bringing home treats from Arizmendi every day. I'll hear her footsteps on the back stairs, bringing stuff up for us, and then after a little while, if no one else is downstairs, I'll go down. She's luring me out of my cave. My love of pastries and my curiosity about what she's brought are too strong to resist.

Whatever's left when they close, they're free to take. Muffins, croissants, éclairs, loaves of bread. Entire pizzas, and good pizza, with nuts and intriguing cheeses.

Claudia is keeping me fed, helping me gain some weight back. Giving me some sweetness and comfort. Like she knows that even going to the corner, to my Sweet Adeline, feels dangerous, especially when there are such nice pastries here.

And then, even though yesterday when I came down, Claudia was still here, it was okay. I feel safe with her. It's nice to have someone around with more perspective, someone who's been alive for a while. I was even tempted to confide in her…maybe because she's one step removed, downstairs, or maybe because I know she's been through some shit. My problems would probably seem like no big deal to her.

But I let her talk instead. She's feeling overwhelmed by single-parenting. She told me that the other day Ingy came home with her eyebrow pierced and she exploded. I actually heard her yelling, from the attic, but I didn't tell her that. She said she feels like a bad mom. Her own mother, in Argentina, was extremely strict and overprotective, and Claudia resolved to be looser with Ingy, give her more freedom. But now she's a teenager, and Claudia knows she needs to keep her safe, but she doesn't know how. "She doesn't fucking listen to me!" she told me, her hands flying up around her face. "She does what she wants."

Ingy resents her mother for her father leaving. Not having a dad around makes her feel deprived, especially when her friends from Berkeley High have these warm, fuzzy hippies for parents. Claudia said, "She doesn't know, they have problems too. Every family has problems."

We're Ingy's family. I'm one of them now. Claudia told me this, her dark eyes holding mine.

I never expected to form such strong bonds with these people. I hoped, but I thought it was just a dream. It's getting harder and harder to keep my sadness secret.

But don't we all have secret sadnesses? Shouldn't I be allowed to keep mine inside me—where they were born, where they died?

March 31

Asha asked me today to go with her to see her friend's new baby. The one whose birth she came home from all bloody. I had just told her I had no plans for the day.

"No," I said awkwardly. "I don't like babies very much." Which is true.

Asha just looked at me, insulted, as if I had offended her, and her friend, and her friend's baby. I held her stare. I knew, somehow, that I couldn't look away, that if I dropped contact, the world I've built would come crumbling down.

We faced off, not blinking, until finally I couldn't take it anymore and I said okay. There was no graceful way out, and I was afraid if I didn't say yes Asha would pull out some bigger guns, and they would almost certainly be worse.

She was so pleased, she chattered the whole way over to her client's house in North Berkeley, telling me about this big May Day protest she's helping organize, asking me to go with her. I agreed just to not have to argue.

I looked out the window at the storefronts of downtown Berkeley and the Gourmet Ghetto, the eucalyptus trees on the hillside above us shuddering in a violent wind. I scanned the streets for Sean, even as I tried to talk myself down: *How would he know where you are? There's no way. He's not here. It's all in your mind. You're fine.*

We stopped at the Cheese Board for slices—supposedly the best pizza around, but I prefer Arizmendi's. Then we headed up the hill to Jessica's place, the bottom floor of a house with a bay view. Asha carried a few stacks of cloth diapers, flowers, and herbs. I carried two slices of pizza for Jessica.

Jessica has long brown curly hair and smiled at me like she was in a trance. Probably sleep-deprived. I wondered how I looked to her. What if she could somehow pick up on my recently having lost a baby—and worried that my meeting her baby might somehow infect it.

It sounds crazy now, but I was having a slight panic attack or something. Paranoid and deeply introverted to the point of being afraid. But knowing Asha would freak if I made this about me in any way.

I sat in the baby's room, painted the color of Pepto Bismol, and watched as Asha held the baby and asked Jessica about how breastfeeding's going, and a bunch of other stuff I didn't really hear because after a while I kind of left my body. My body was sitting in the special rocking chair for nursing, which goes forward and back, rather than up and down. But I was looking down at all of it from the ceiling.

Jessica was changing the baby out of a disposable diaper and into one of the cloth ones. The baby was kicking her little legs, and Jessica pulled out a new outfit she wanted to show Asha: a little yellow shorts and sweater set that someone had knitted. She put the clothes on the baby, and a little bow in her hair. That clearly made Asha uncomfortable and I could see her bite her tongue.

I was just sitting over on the side, rocking. I watched myself but wasn't able to make myself move, other than the manic rocking forward and back, the chair addictive in its trance-inducing movement. As if I was going forward and back through time, time changed and I watched it from above. I thought for a moment that maybe the baby saw me there, she was looking right at me and seemed to be waving her pudgy little hand.

But then all of a sudden it was like I had been dropped back down into the chair, I fell back into myself, and a terrible alarm started going off throughout my whole system, like the time in the kitchen when I was making the tofu burgers but worse, my whole body shaking and my ears ringing.

Sweating suddenly, and dizzy, I excused myself and made it to Jessica's bathroom just in time to vomit up the gross corn pizza. I almost passed out, lay my head on the cold tile floor, which felt so good against my sweaty skin. I watched the eucalyptus outside the window, storming in the wind.

After a while I cooled off and calmed down. But all I wanted was to stay there on that soothing floor forever and watch the trees dance and not think about a thing.

Now it's later in the day and I can't stop thinking about what happened. It feels like a dream. Did I imagine the whole thing?

Was it just being around a newborn? Now that I'm finally sort of dealing, or at least thinking about what happened, I can't handle it head-on, I have to float up to the ceiling, remove myself from the scene?

Just thinking of it, I feel nauseous again. What is happening? I feel like I'm sliding into some dark place in myself, like Alice down the rabbit hole. And oh, man, I do not want to know what's down there.

April 4

A 7.2, 89-second quake shook northwest Mexico and Southern California this afternoon. It was the strongest earthquake felt in SoCal in at least 18 years.

April 8

Brix and Lily are building a house in his backyard, a cob house made from mud and straw. Ingy and I went to help them yesterday. I needed to get out of this fucking house, out of my mind.

It was so nice to be outside. The weather is warming up, all the flowers are blooming. We took a bus past Fruitvale then got out and walked another half-mile or so to Brix's. It's so different over there from where we live—more industrial, and strongly Latino, with lots of panaderías and piñata shops.

Ingy took it all in with interest. She hasn't been outside our neighborhood much and said Fruitvale reminded her of Buenos Aires, where Claudia's from, and where Ingy visited once, when she was 10.

We passed a new soccer field with bright green grass, then turned onto a smaller street, winding our way toward his place. And then suddenly I saw in front of me the SPCA where I adopted Moonshine so many years ago, when I lived in S.F. I had forgotten all about it until I saw the structure standing in front of me.

I stopped short and just stared. Realizing where I was, my body flooding with memories. This has happened a few times since being back—experiencing the East Bay, which itself is different, through different eyes. I've changed, and it's changed, and the result is a confusing combination of nostalgia and disorientation—like I've been blindfolded, turned in circles for years, and the blindfold removed. I was reminded, seeing the shelter, of that old me, how I felt here then, so much lighter. I had the strange feeling that it was actually a different city, a different story, a parallel universe. I'm a different character now.

I haven't wanted to think about my dog, to have to deal with my guilt for leaving him behind, for not going to get him from my parents since I've been back. Going to get him would mean seeing them, and telling them I live here now, so I just left him on the list of things I'm not thinking about. These years away from him, I've turned cold to other dogs, for the first time in my life. I ignore them on the street, not petting them like I used to, not even looking at them.

I wasn't up for telling Ingy about my history with the shelter. Instead I asked her if she wanted to go in.

I knew she did. Claudia told me recently that Ingy has been begging for a dog for her 14th birthday, which is a couple months away. Claudia told her no, but she told me that secretly she's considering it. She thinks Ingy is probably old enough to care for a dog herself now, and that the responsibility would be good for her. She'd need to be home from school by a certain time to let the dog out, up by a certain time to feed it. She'd need to train it, maybe even help pay for its food. Playing in our backyard with a puppy would be much more wholesome than hanging out on Telegraph Avenue, getting pierced for kicks. Maybe a dog would keep Ingy off drugs!

We pushed open the door that read DOGS, walked through another set of doors, and then headed out to the dogs in their outdoor enclosures. Most of the dogs came running up to us and Ingy looked stricken by their small quarters, by how many there were and their sounds of longing. Sometimes I have to remind myself that Ingy is only a girl—she looks and acts so much older. And though she has sophisticated taste, and hangs out with us comfortably, she's actually not wise in all the ways of the world, which is a good thing.

We walked further down the aisle, until Ingy crossed in front of me to a small dog a couple cages away, which looked like a beagle terrier mix.

Unlike the other dogs, it seemed pretty independent. When Ingy said hi in a raised voice, it blinked and looked over at her, but didn't move from where it was. It was a little scruff of a thing that was aloof and goofy, just like her, a little bit punk rock, just like her. She said it reminded her of a dog in one of her favorite mangas, named Sosuke.

"That's the name of a famous Samurai warrior," I told her. "So that seems apt for this little guy." I smiled.

She smiled back uncertainly.

"He does look pretty tough," I said. "He must be to survive in here."

Again, she looked up at me, eyebrows rising as her forehead furrowed.

"In the slammer with all these big bad criminals," I explained. "Though he doesn't look too innocent, probably in here for something more serious than we'd think."

She caught on and joined in. "Yeah, like maybe drug-dealing," she said.

"Yeah, or something a little more highbrow, like maybe he's a card shark or something, pulling schemes on casinos. Some hussy must have turned him in."

"Yeah. He's too smart to get caught." She nodded. She stood up and saw the tag on his cage. "Oh my god, it says his name is Sharky!"

"Ha!" I laughed. "Are you serious?" I walked over to the cage, and saw that she was right. Unbelievable. It also said that he was about 5 and had been found without tags or a chip, walking nearby a few weeks before.

Right here was where I had given my dog his name. His white-gray coat reminded me of the moon's surface.

Even matted and dirty it still had a gloss to it, enticing me to pet him. Glowing like the moon itself.

I was remembering that dogs need people, and vice versa.

I put my arm around Ingy and said, "We should get to Brix's. Goodbye, Sharky. Fare thee well."

"Bye, Sharky," she said sadly.

Sharky looked up, then went back to nonchalantly grooming himself. I stealthily took note of his adoption info, and followed Ingy out.

The cob construction was like a Hippunks Gone Wild episode. Lily in her bra and shorts, stomping about in the mud, getting covered in it. It felt incredible, using mud and straw and wood and our hands to make something—something Brix is going to live in.

Merry was there, and we talked a little. She was even nicer than at the Starry Plough. She has these giant blue eyes that look they're taking in all of life. She is, like, the opposite of depressed. I want to feel that way again.

She took a break from building for a while and played some music, some stuff of her own. She and Brix have a recording studio in their garage, and she's getting a few songs together for a solo LP. She sang a new song called "Brix's Chickens." They're hers too, she just likes how it sounds. He made them a mini cob coop as practice for the house.

April 15

Yet another big earthquake today, a 6.9 this time. In Qinghai, China, where the population is mostly Tibetan. Once again, hundreds are dead and injured, homeless.

I look at pictures of the monks out looking for victims buried under the rubble, searching for dead strangers.

I should be able to look at the stuff I've buried in my own body. I'm alive. I have no responsibilities, other than to get better. I should be able to do this.

April 22

10:20 a.m.

I don't feel like celebrating my birthday. I don't want to go out, and I don't want to ask anyone to do anything for me here. No one knows it's today, so I can just boycott it.

I feel like staying in bed, and since it's my birthday, that's what I'm going to do. Sadie will keep me company.

I'm flailing here, Sadie. What am I doing? What kind of life is this, hiding in an attic? I can't survive on this.

At least I'm fucking 30. I am so ready to leave my 20s behind.

1:40 p.m.

I took my last Vicodin, my birthday gift to myself. It's helping me feel like spending my birthday alone in the attic isn't such a terrible thing. It reminds me of those last few days in Japan, and my first week or so here, so high I floated above it all, just skimmed the surface. Nothing hurt, nothing could hurt me, no hurt could matter. I needed it then, during that weird limbo, and I needed it today.

If I had gone to my check-up after the miscarriage, I could have gotten more Vicodin. I could have fixed whatever has rotted inside me. Now it's too late. I know I should go to the doctor and see what's wrong…but I don't want to know.

Wish I could have food delivered to my room. The delivery guy could scale the palm tree and I could pop out the screen and trade him money for food. Thai food, maybe, mmm…

Meantime it's PB&J, sandwich of depression. At least it's good peanut butter, the chunky fresh stuff from the

Berkeley Bowl. And yummy organic blueberry jam. The bread is good too, a brioche loaf. I'm not suffering too much.

Maybe I'll buy myself some clothes with the gift card my parents sent.

It's been surprisingly liberating to have so little stuff here—I could still pack everything into those three suitcases if I have to leave again.

7:11 p.m.

Clara found me on Facebook! Under my new name. She's such a clever devil. She knew I'd dreamed of visiting Nara, and put it together with my middle name, and voilà, there I was, Nara Allison. She wanted to wish me Happy Birthday.

It was so good to hear from her, though my heart was racing when I opened her message. Being found definitely quickens the heart. It reminded me that there's a world out there, one that contains the place I left.

She said that Sean had been in touch with her and that he left Japan in March, to stay with his brother in L.A. She said he was planning to keep working with his dad's law firm, would still be traveling a lot, would just be based in L.A. instead. She said he'd been hurt, but that he didn't seem angry at me.

We've been chatting on Facebook, and it's making me miss her so much. That deep closeness, the ease of an old friend. We've known each other 22 years, since that ballet class we both hated, when we bonded hiding in the bathroom. It all happened so fast, my leaving, I didn't think about how hard it would be to not have her in my life.

She asked if I'm going to work with kids again. I told her no.

She likes my new name. She says she wishes she could

give herself a new name. Her roots in Japan are so deep with her clients and friends, it would be too much work to start over like that. I think she might be kind of jealous that I got to start fresh, from scratch. That I'm here. Her life there is good, but I know she misses California.

I only told her a bit about my life here. She wanted to know more, but I don't want to tell Clara about my lies, I doubt she'll understand.

I gave her my address. I know she won't give it to Sean, and it seems safe now that he's gone. She's going to send me some more green tea, and a birthday present, and a Princess Mononoke charm from the Totoro store for Ingy's birthday. And the box I left with her.

Japan has officially flooded back in. Maybe I am strong enough to handle it now. Less fragile and afraid.

I don't have to feel bad about myself. It's not helping.

Clara cared enough about me to find me. She said she just had a feeling, and we've been psychic together all our lives, so I'm not surprised. I need her now, so the universe brought her to me.

April 24

Asha made ramen for me tonight.

She remembered I was a Taurus, and she asked me when my birthday was, and when I told her she felt terrible that they'd missed it. I told her what I'd wanted for my birthday was sleep, but she wanted to do something to make up for it. So when she asked me if I was missing anything from Japan, I told her I was missing noodles.

She made delicious ramen, with a miso base, and fried tofu, shiitake mushrooms, corn, scallion, carrots. And plum wine.

I cried a little when I tasted it. Kind of embarrassing, but whatever. Asha was so happy that I was downstairs, and eating. She tried to hide her smile as she slurped her noodles, and I tried to hide my tears.

May 1

I checked my bank balance today. I've been afraid to look, have been avoiding looking at my statements and my balance. I finally just made myself do it.

I have $6,112 after my May rent check goes through. Rent/utilities for the rest of the year will be $4,200, which leaves me with only $1,912 for everything else. Which means I have to get a job soon.

I truly have no idea what to do for work. I've only ever worked with kids, and that's the one thing I now don't want to do. I could wait tables or something, I guess, but it feels scary to be so visible.

Maybe I'll see if Lily has any ideas. They think I'm starting at Mills in the fall but it makes sense I would want something part-time until then.

Talking to Asha about it is probably not a good idea. Today was the protest in S.F. that I had agreed to go to with her, against the new Arizona immigration law. It's embarrassing, but I've never been to a protest, and I was too scared. When I told her I didn't feel up to it she got really mad.

"God, you're so selfish!" she said, her hands in fists at her side. "People out there have real problems. Why don't you think about them for a change?"

"That's a good question," I told her. "That's a really good question."

And maybe she thought I was being sarcastic, but I wasn't. Her jaw dropped open and she said, "I'll stop inviting you to stuff. Clearly you don't want to do anything."

I started to argue with that, but what could I say? She's right.

She grabbed her sign, which said MAY DAY, MAY DAY!

RACISM IS NOT REFORM, and she stomped down the stairs, slammed the front door behind her.

I'm glad I didn't go, because things got ugly with the cops. That's nothing for her but it would have been too much for me. Though maybe she's right—maybe it would do me good to get caught up in some real problems for a change.

May 5

We're having a naked party.

Lily proposed it to Asha and me at our house meeting. "I wanna have a clothes-swapping party," she said. "Also known as a naked party. We go through our clothes and pull out whatever we're done with, our friends come over with their donated clothes, and then we all get naked and try stuff on and end up with a bunch of new stuff." I wasn't sure about getting naked with strangers, but a party sounded like a chance to be social without having to leave the house.

She said, "You guys should invite whoever you want. I already talked to a few people about it. I was thinking next Thursday night, what do you think?"

Asha and I exchanged looks. Sometimes Lily, in her excitement, forgets to check in with us before making plans.

Asha spoke up. "You know, Lil, sometimes it's like you forget we live here too."

"Oh," Lily said, subdued.

Asha looked at me, raised her eyebrows like, *Your turn.* I just looked back at her. She widened her eyes at me, shook her head, and then said to Lily, "It would be nice if next time you checked with us first, before inviting a bunch of people over."

"Okay," Lily said.

"And, you know, a week isn't really enough advance notice. I happen to be available Thursday, unless something comes up at the shelter."

"Okay, good." I could tell Lily was biting her tongue against a sharper response. She and Asha seem to be trying to keep their tempers in check around me.

They looked at me. "I like the idea, and Thursday's fine for me too. Who are you inviting? Anyone foxy?"

Lily grinned. "Sure, let me think about it. Asha, anyone in particular you want to see naked?"

Asha was too cool to say so, but I knew there was a red-headed friend of Lily's that she thought was cute. I decided to try and make it up to Asha for not stepping in to help with Lily. "Lily, what about that redhead friend of yours? What's her name? She was here for Claudia's birthday...?"

"Terra, you mean? She's a total fox." Lily really should be queer. Sometimes I think, *Not yet she's not.*

"Yeah, her. The red fox."

"Good one. Yeah, she's Brix's friend, from the garden." Brix and Lily volunteer at Spiral Garden, an urban farm near here, that's where they met. "I'm working there on Tuesday, I'll see if she's into it."

I glanced at Asha, sitting next to me, inspecting the couch.

"Cool, yeah, let's do it!" I said, changing the subject. "I may need help going through my clothes, though—it's pretty bare bones up there."

"Well, good, you'll get some new clothes. And it's fun to see your stuff on other people. I say, if you haven't worn it in a year..." She mimed a jump shot. "Toss! I went to a naked party and got a ton of stuff. These boots, actually." Sitting in the antique chair with the red cushion, she ran her hand lovingly up her leg, caressing her black lace-up boots.

"We should definitely have drinks," Asha said moodily.

"Hell, yeah," Lily agreed. "The mint out back is out of control, we can make mojitos."

"Mmm, mojitos," I said longingly. "Just women, right?"

"Yeah, I don't want no guys here checking out all the naked ladies," Asha said.

"No, Asha, we'll leave that to you," Lily said. Asha couldn't suppress a little smile at that one. "You know I'm looking out for you."

"Oh, Lil, I can take care of my own love life, thank you very much," Asha retorted.

"Can you?" Lily asked. "I haven't seen you with any ladies since you decided to be a dyke."

"Well, *give* me a few weeks, okay?" Asha smiled.

"What about you?" Lily asked me. "How's the dating going?"

"Um, it's not," I said sheepishly.

"Dating sucks," Lily said. "I'm so glad I never have to do it again." She twirled around the living room like a little girl playing ballerina. "Bye!" she said and twirled out of the room.

"See, that's why I'm glad I'm not straight anymore," Asha said.

Later, looking for the broom, I opened Lily's door, not expecting her to be there, and found her and Brix sleeping. Sunlight from the window covered their bottom halves like a blanket. She was on her back, and he was curled into her, on his side, his head fitting perfectly under her armpit, the locks at her neck curling around his fine brown mullet, his arm across her chest holding her hand. His leg was curved around hers, the top of his foot against her other calf.

I froze, surprised and terrified of disturbing them. They were so perfectly entangled. Like they loved each other so much, they wanted as many of their body parts as possible to be touching, even in sleep.

Blessed by the light of her yellow room, they were like a picture of love. I didn't covet it, and I wasn't envious of

Brix. I just buckled that image away in my heart.

As I slowly closed the door behind me, I wondered what they were making in their dreams together…another world, their next place.

May 12, Willow's due date

I drove Lily's Subaru to Muir Beach today to mark the day. It was as close as I could get to her.

There were almost no people on the beach, in the middle of the day on a Tuesday. I walked down to the water, rolled up my jeans, and waded in, staring out toward Japan for a long time. A big wave came in and then the water was up around my hips. It felt good to get numb in the place where she'd lived.

Finally I got out of the water, and I found a stick and carved *Willow* into the wet sand, in cursive, like I did on Yuigahama beach on New Year's. Then I walked around and around it, dragging the stick around and around, my wet jeans dripping a ring of seawater around her name, making a bigger and bigger circle until I finally walked away.

She left me. My little seahorse left me. It was just the universe fucking with me, making me think I could ever care for anyone else. It was just as likely to end in death as in love.

I climbed a big rock and looked out over the ocean. I imagined Frida Kahlo as Freeda, a mermaid swimming to me, her long, dark hair twisted down her back with seaweed. Her tail made of sequiny scales, blue and green and in-between, and her face ashen, serious. She was coming for me, to take me to Willow. Willow would have been waiting for me, she would have forgiven me, and together we'd live in the waves.

Ocean waves only feel like the universe splitting open when you're on land. Out there in the center I might finally learn to let go, to float.

If she'd stayed with me, what place would there have been for us, here on land?

Sail away, just sail away, Nara…you have that whole blue landscape to escape to when life on land is too much. Just close your eyes, and sail away.

This is what I told myself when the sunset was over and the cold came, and I had no wood for a fire, and my whole body shook with shivers under my wet jeans, but leaving her felt impossible.

I don't belong here on land. I belong out there with my seahorse, with the pirates and the mermaids.

May 13

Asha came up today and helped me weed out some stuff to pass on at the Naked Party tonight. Too-cute tops that I'm over and jeans that don't fit anymore. She got me stoned as I tried on the stuff I wasn't sure about.

Then we went downstairs and did the same for her. She wants a new look, and I got all excited, clapping my hands and saying "Makeover!!!" à la *Clueless*. She gave me a deadly look at that. But it was nice to hang out with her again, to be frivolous and have fun. I even did her hair for her, spiky on top and smooth on the sides. We put together an outfit for the party too. Her clothes are pretty boring, but we'll find her some new stuff.

She wouldn't let me put any makeup on her. She thinks she needs to be more butch now that she wants to get with the ladies. Every item of her clothing with a flower on it is now sitting in our living room. I told her there are lots of women who will love her just the way she is.

I asked her what she's looking for and she said she wasn't really sure. "Shaggy hair," she said. "I like shaggy hair."

Lily has confirmed that the redhead Terra will be here, as well as a bunch of other people I don't know, including a new neighbor who just moved into the house next door— not the crack house, but the one on the other side.

May 14

10:24 a.m.

What was I thinking, making a date for 10:30 this morning? I was drunk, so I wasn't thinking. And I didn't want to be away from her any longer than I had to.

Her! Yes, her! More soon about her.

Meantime, ow. Boy do I wish I still had one more Vicodin.

I'm nervous she won't like me in the light of day. I do have new clothes to wear, at least.

Dress over jeans, T-shirt over dress, sweater over T-shirt. And pink Converse. Anything would look good with these shoes.

6:44 p.m.

She just left, and already I want her back. But first, before I forget, I better report back about the Naked Party.

Start at the beginning. The pitcher of mojitos I made before everyone got there, sampling as I went, relaxing me. Getting naked with a bunch of strangers was a slightly nerve-racking concept. On the other hand, I was excited about new clothes, and relieved to be done with all the psycho attic stuff lately. So I resolved to not be a freak, and enjoy.

It is my house too, after all. Sometimes it might not feel like it, since I haven't lived here long, but for the party I cleaned *both* bathrooms. Cleaning a toilet gives one a real feeling of ownership. Knowing Asha was nervous helped too.

We had organized our stuff into sections—shirts, skirts, dresses, pants, sweaters, coats and jackets. A bookshelf for accessories and shoes. It was like having a thrift shop in our living room. My neglected femme felt very satisfied.

"Lily, you're brilliant," I told her. "Shopping from the comfort of our own home, for free. And with drinks! And snacks!"

She turned on some Fela Kuti then did a little Lily dance. Running in place, with some booty-shaking.

"Are there any butches coming?" Asha asked. She shot a challenge stare at Lily, blinking under her glasses. "Or is it gonna be all girly stuff?"

In response, Lily bumped Asha with her hip, and Asha bumped her back—but Asha's was a bit half-hearted. I thought, *I can do better than that.* I'm constantly having these weird competitive thoughts around Lily.

"Hmm," Lily said, mulling over Asha's challenge, "one of my friends who's not coming dropped off some butchy stuff…and the neighbor next door is pretty butch. When I met her on the street the other day, I thought she was a guy at first."

I froze. My stomach did a somersault. "What does she look like?" I asked. And then the doorbell rang. We looked at each other and laughed.

"You'll see soon enough!" Lily called as she trundled down the stairs.

And it was her. Our first guest. My stomach did more acrobatics. She was cute.

She was wearing all black: T-shirt, Dickies, and boots. One arm was covered in a sleeve of tattoos. I was staring at the geisha there when Lily introduced me—July is her name.

"Hey," I said. "Nice tattoos."

"Thanks," she said and smiled. She has the tough-butch stance I have a weakness for, a filling up of space that implies confidence. But she also seemed a little shy, which was endearing.

"Come have a drink," I said. "You like mojitos?"

"I do," she said. The first time July told me "I do."

"Tell me how this is, it might need more agave."

She sipped it and said, "More rum."

I smiled and added a healthy pour of rum, poured her another taste.

"Mmm," she said and nodded. Her hair, longer than most butches' around these parts, is dark brown and soft, and was falling over her black-frame glasses, behind which big beautiful yellow-brown eyes looked right into me. I looked back into them and got lost for a moment, forgot where I was. The alcohol had gone to my head.

I recovered quickly, poured myself another, filled hers up, added a sprig of mint to both. Leaned back against the kitchen counter and held my glass in front of me, like a shield. She was exactly as tall as me, in those boots, from that position.

"July," I said. "That's a cool name."

"Thanks. I changed it about a year ago."

"It suits you. What was your name before?"

"Oh, I can't tell you that," she said with a smile, moving just slightly toward me.

I smiled back, disarmed. "I just changed my name too." I hadn't told my roommates this, that my name is new, and for a second I panicked. Then I reminded myself, *Relax.* "Mine's an homage to Nara—the city in Japan."

"Oh, wow—because of the big Buddha there? I've always wanted to see him. What's he like?"

"Amazing." She was so excited, so receptive, the lie slipped out of my mouth before I could stop it. Because of course I don't know that the Nara Daibutsu is amazing, since I've never been. But it was too late to backtrack. *Nobody knows anything about you other than what you tell them. It's fine.* "I'm new to the neighborhood too. I just came from Japan a few months ago."

"Oh, wow. I'm dying to go to Japan. Did you love it?"

"I loved it, and hated it." I smiled. "I got this there." I pulled up the black-and-white striped T-shirt I was wearing, an old one of Asha's that we'd decided was too big for her, and I showed her the pink flower around my belly button. "Sakura. They blossom and the country goes crazy."

Her eyes rested on my tattoo, then lazily dipped a little lower for a second. I was wearing some new jeans I'd snagged as I was organizing the piles. They may be a little too tight, but July didn't seem to mind.

She pulled up the sleeve of her T-shirt to show me a big sakura on the underside of her upper arm, about the size of mine, and some smaller ones interspersed along the geisha. "I've seen the ones in D.C., but a whole country full of them…wow."

"Are you coming from D.C.?"

"No, I grew up near there. I'm coming from New Orleans. My friend had a room opening in her place next door, and I was ready for a change so I went for it."

"You're gonna love it. We can explore together." I couldn't believe what was flying out of my mouth. "Check out our backyard," I said, taking her from the kitchen to the back porch, and its view of the surrounding houses. "That's yours?" I asked, pointing at the neighboring yard.

"Yeah," she said. "The magnolia tree makes me feel at home. We had one at our house in New Orleans."

"I love that tree. I was sad when it lost its flowers. I sit here a lot, and I like to face your yard, since over there they have barking dogs and other shady stuff going on."

She looked concerned. "Nothing too extreme, don't worry. They're just loud, and I live in the attic, right above their stoop. Claudia downstairs—I'll introduce you, she's great—says it's a crack house. But she's lived here a long time and apparently they've never caused any major problems."

"I had drug-dealer neighbors at my last house."

"Well, you'll feel right at home then. Where's your room?" She pointed to the front of the house.

We sat down on the porch bench. I pulled my knees up, facing her and her backyard, and she sat Indian-style, facing me and my backyard. I guessed from her excellent posture, and her interest in the Nara Daibutsu, that maybe she's Buddhist.

The condensation from our glasses dripped on us. It was warm out, a good day to get naked. I was barefoot, my toenails a rosy pink, my lips too.

I got the chips and guacamole from the kitchen and brought them out to the porch. Some people had come in and my roommates were chatting with them in the living room.

"This guac is good," July said with her mouth full. "It's so California."

"Pretty hot geisha you got there," I said, nodding at the tattoo running almost the length of her right arm. "Hey, where are your clothes?" I asked, realizing July had come in empty-handed.

"I just pared everything way down before I moved, so I don't have anything, sorry," July said. "And I didn't think to bring any food, either...but I'll run to the store for booze when we get low, yeah?"

"Okay. Wanna go in?" I asked. "There might be something for you—Lily's butch friend donated some stuff even though she couldn't come."

July smiled. "Whenever. I'm enjoying sitting here with you."

I wondered if she knew I was into women, or if she was always this confident. Then it occurred to me that maybe Lily had told her—maybe Lily had set this whole thing up.

Lily knew exactly what I was looking for.

I am such a sucker.

I gulped my drink, and got up to pour us another. "Do you smoke?" I asked.

"Sometimes."

"Wanna share one?"

"Sure." I got an American Spirit from the kitchen drawer, lit it, and passed it over to her with what I hoped was a cavalier gaze.

"Don't worry, I don't bite," she said and grinned.

"Did Lily mention I'm queer?" I asked, surprising myself again. Wanting some control in our butch-femme dance.

"She mentioned you were wanting to date women," July said, hitting the nail on the head in a maddening way. The implication, of course, was that I wasn't queer, not yet. Or at least in my paranoia that's what I thought.

"My other roommate, Asha, is too. She has a little crush on someone who's coming tonight." Again, I couldn't believe I'd said that out loud. The rum was truth serum! I put my finger to my lips, indicating that this was our little secret. July put her finger to her lips too.

We were quiet. I looked down at my toes, wondering if my cheeks were pink too, wondering if what seemed to be happening was really happening. Just an hour ago, she was over there, and I was over here, and now we were both here, looking over there…my mojito brain couldn't do the math.

I gave up. "I wonder if she's here yet. Asha's crush girl," I whispered. "We should go find out. She's got red hair."

"Okay," July whispered back, putting our cigarette out in the tin Yellowstone ashtray. "Vamos."

8 p.m.

OK, I made myself some food, to sustain me for the rest of the story. Got a text from July saying she misses me. I was tempted to tell her to come back, but I need to finish getting this down first.

The Naked Party. So many great moments. I wish I could just plug Sadie into my head and download them directly.

Drunken dress-up is what it was, a bunch of half-naked women getting high on one another. The smell of female sex, an intoxicating orange blossom, intensified with the night. That's where real life beats movies and books—the smell.

Lily played Donna Summer, Marvin Gaye, the Bee Gees. We left just the twinkle lights on in the living room and a few candles burning, propped the full-length mirror over near the light in the kitchen.

Lily had brought in all the scissors in the house, and her sewing machine. Socks became gloves, sweaters became leg-warmers, skirts became miniskirts…

"Up with upcycling!" Lily shouted, pumping her fist in the air. We were her band of ragamuffins, jam jars of mojitos instead of goblets of wine.

For the first time since I got here, I was completely in my element. I made some cool stuff, but mostly I had fun playing matchmaker. I got to know the clothes and would hand-pick the right person for them, instead of the other way around. Some lonely, lovely dress would have been not quite right for anyone, almost forgotten until the perfect person for it walked in. I'd present the dress, request that they try it on, and they'd drop their pants.

It was a bonding experience—total strangers were collaborators within minutes. Nine times out of ten I nailed it. I was trying to place this beautiful floor-length patchwork skirt all night, until Merry walked in late and I made her strip down to her apricot cotton undies. She has an adorable bum, and the skirt hugged it perfectly.

We were all stripping down, even Asha. Surprisingly sexy in her purple tank top and black boy-cut underwear, she'd been shy at first but then seemed to start to revel in the freedom of it. The drunker she got the closer she got to Terra, until she was in Terra's lap.

Terra reminds me of Tilda Swinton, that long graceful neck and the red hair, mixed with Claire Danes, the young, beautiful face and intelligent eyes. She's only 23. She said she changed the spelling of her name from Tara to Terra when she was in high school, because she's always loved digging in the dirt. I love that I'm not the only one with a new name.

I like her. She only wears clean, fitted lines, she said. Nothing remotely femmey. Under her clothes she wore a white ribbed tank top over her flat chest, and atop her head a bowler. She and Asha were so picky, I was determined to find stuff for them, wheedling out their preferences. They'd burrowed into a spot on the couch and were fully engaged in getting to know each other. Finally I left them to it.

I was the polar opposite of Terra and Asha—a total slut. I tried on almost every dress there, July carefully averting her eyes as I undressed, at least at first. I wore the gray lace bralette and panties I had splurged on in Tokyo, cheeks peeking out. I felt self-conscious at first, but after I got used to it I didn't mind the eyes on me. I would try something on, check myself out in the mirror, ask July or Lily yes or no if I was unsure. My yes pile was much bigger than anyone else's.

July got into the spirit of the thing too. Her black boxers out above a too-big pair of jeans that hung almost to her knees, she did a hilarious spider-walk around the living room, cracking us all up. She's a flirt, I could tell, but she was flirting almost exclusively with me, so it was okay. She's a good dancer, slyly looking off in the distance as she shakes her hips. I asked where she got her moves, and she said from watching *Soul Train* as a kid with her brother.

"What's *Soul Train*?" one of our delightful young guests asked, and July took the end of a string of lights dangling down and held them at her hip, swinging them in a circle as she said, "The Souuuuuuul Train." We started a soul train through the house then, collecting cars as we went.

"Hoo, hoo!" I called like a train whistle.

"Hooa, hooa!" July called like a clubgoer.

Lily showed me how to use her sewing machine, as she did alterations. Calling myself The Accessorizer, I brought neglected jewelry, hats, shoes, belts, scarves around the room, completing outfits. For every successful placement, Lily and I would high-five, or do a hip bump, a proper one. The original categorized piles shrunk and new individual piles grew.

Several stripteases and lap dances were performed—with so many clothes coming on and off, it was inevitable. Our parts were no longer private. It seemed like everyone was scamming on someone, except Lily, who was busy managing rejects like a captivating sales associate. I only saw her try on a couple things, caught a glimpse of her striped undies, her small breasts free. She was also possibly the only straight girl there, and she'd probably engineered every one of the hookups herself.

She caught my eye once after I'd been batting my lashes at July and raised her eyebrows suggestively. I shook my head at her, then couldn't resist toppling her over onto the couch, creating a drunken pileup of half-naked bodies. Asha was wearing Terra's hat and playing with her short red hair, a look of awe on her face, and hardly noticed the arrival of new bodies on the couch next to them.

The room held steady at a dozen or more, some leaving with their stash, others taking their place. If I hadn't been so busy, I would have loved to sit and watch, like I used to. Each one was beautiful, completely distinct from all the others, and yet their comfort in their bodies, lack of pretense, and earthy look and smell made them seem the same. Some a little more hippie, some a little more punk, but none straight up one or the other.

Asha brought out the weed, and someone hooked up a strobe light that had been donated. I danced when the music made me. July came up behind me once, held my hips as we moved together to Prince.

It was sweet to be digging on someone but also aware of everyone else, getting to know July within the shared experience. The old me would have immersed myself in her, like Terra and Asha, ignoring everything around me. But now I like the idea of a relationship within a community. Because I know it's the community that will catch me if I fall.

The pitcher of mojitos was emptied and filled three times. July and I walked to the liquor store for more rum and smokes. On the way, I asked about her love life.

"I had a long-term girlfriend in New Orleans, but

that's been over for a while." She grinned at me. It looked like an invitation.

We went into the store and picked the more expensive of the two brands of rum, asked for American Spirits, and July handed over the cash, wouldn't accept any from me.

"No, man, I'm so glad you guys invited me over. So glad," she said, and held my gaze. Our eyes were, like, magnetized. In my peripheral vision I felt the counter guy looking back and forth between the two of us. I pulled my eyes away from hers and gave him a big cheesy grin.

Outside, she handed me the smokes, and I stopped to pack them, so we could have one on the walk home. She said, "I like your bangs."

"They need a trim. I'm missing my stylist in Japan." I remembered she'd told me she did hair. "Hey, maybe you can be my new stylist!"

"I'm a barber, actually. But of course I can do your bangs. Though I think your bangs are perfect. You're kind of perfect."

She was back in her original black ensemble, and standing there in front of the Alcatraz Liquor Store she looked like James Dean, but more substantial. Brave enough to turn over the upper hand. Something Dani had never, not once, done in our year together. James Dean probably never did either.

"I'm a mess." I was wearing a new-to-me gold lamé vintage dress that fits perfectly but is far too fancy for a walk to the liquor store, the pink Converse slightly too tight on my feet, makeup long gone, ponytail half-fallen-out from trying on clothes all night. It was 11, and we'd been at it since 6, when July arrived.

"You're a perfect mess," she replied, setting the rum on the sidewalk next to her.

I tried to tap a cigarette from the pack, in a cool response to her compliment, and dropped the pack in the process. I bent down to pick them up and when I stood back up, my head spun. July steadied me, and I looked at her, dizzy for a second. She held my forearms, steadied me, and then pulled me closer and kissed me.

I held her head in my hands, and her hair was so, so soft. It had been a succulent night for the senses, and now there was a climax happening on Alcatraz Avenue. I felt the softness of her hair and of her tongue in my mouth, her hands behind me, reaching up my back. I had dropped the smokes again.

9:15 p.m.

I finally gave in and texted July to come over. She'll be here soon, so I have to finish.

After everyone left last night, around midnight, July helped us bag up the orphan clothes to donate. I wanted her to stay, but I was pretty trashed so we made our date for much too early this morning at Sweet Ad's.

As I walked out of the front gate this morning, it slammed behind me, and I looked left and saw July walk out at the same moment. We laughed together, a similar short burst, and my fears were gone, just like that. I walked up to her and kissed her.

"Hi," I said. "How you feeling?" I put my arms around her waist.

"Hurting a little. But happy. You?" She put her arms around me.

"Me too." I smiled into her eyes, my puffy eyes covered by new cat-eye sunglasses. "It's nice to see you. Neighbor." She took my hand, and I steered her in the right direction, toward the corner a block up. "Pretty cool. Not only are you my next-door neighbor, this is our local café. You do like pastries, right?"

"I love pastries."

She stopped walking, turned to me, and pushed the glasses up onto my head. She looked at me carefully, then said, "But I'd go anywhere with you."

I was shaken by her intensity, and by the feeling of being looked at so closely, when I felt I looked so unalluring. I said, "Well, great, let's go to Sweet Adeline!" I pulled my glasses back over my eyes.

She smiled at me like I was a kid whose strange behavior she understood perfectly. I had the uncomfortable feeling that she understood me better than I did.

She asked, "You okay?"

I felt then, for the first time, the irritation of being with someone who could see me, really see who I was. This thing I've been so desperately wanting…when I finally got it, all I wanted was to run back up to my attic and be alone. Not go sit in a café with this stranger who could read me like a book.

"I'm okay," I said, not even able to bring myself to smile. "Let's go in."

She looked a little bewildered but followed me in, her hand resting on my lower back. I felt it there, and a resistance to being supported. I moved up to the pastry case, just far enough that her hand fell away.

I pointed out my favorites, then walked away from her to place my order. Glancing back as I went to pay, I caught a look from her, like, *Wonderful, this one's got issues.* And I knew then that I did. And I didn't want to scare her off with them.

I found a table, took off my sunglasses, started drinking

my coffee. By the time July joined me I had talked myself down. I said, "Sorry if I seem weird. I'm a little nervous." I looked at her wistfully. "That shirt looks really good on you." She'd snagged a sunflower-yellow T-shirt last night that highlighted the yellow in her eyes. She wore a thick brown cardigan over it, and the big jeans, still hanging down over her boxers, but with a belt to keep them up.

She smiled and warmed her hands on her compostable cup, and I smiled back. Our food was brought to us, and we were back to being budding soul mates. I couldn't believe how close I'd come to fucking it up.

We started telling each other our stories. She's 40, has had a few long-term girlfriends, and seems pretty healthy. She didn't talk much about her family, and neither did I. I sketched a rough outline, tried not to worry what would happen when we got to the stuff I can't talk about. I won't want to lie to her. *Slowly, slowly,* I reminded myself.

We finished our quiche and agreed it was the best quiche the world has ever known. To go, I got a chocolate chip cookie and a cheddar and chive scone, and she got a roasted bell pepper galette and a slice of carrot bread. Our biggest concern now was whether we'd go back to her house, or mine.

We went up to the attic, had one long, slow kiss, and lay in my bed staring at each other till we fell asleep. I woke up a couple hours later and found her next to me in bed, still asleep. I lay there and watched her for a while, learning her face, its softness in sleep, without her glasses. When she woke up to find me staring at her, I was embarrassed but I distracted her with more kisses. She's a really good kisser, and she held my head in her hand, like I was something special.

I made us some tea and we shared the rest of our pastries. Then she left to take a shower at her place and I got up to write it all down.

She's coming in the front door. The gymnastics are back.

May 16

What if I found her, Sadie? The one I've been waiting for.
Is that what's happening, could it be?
    Oh my god, it feels so good to just fall in.

May 17

July just went to rent us a movie, and the bubble we've been living in popped. When she leaves, even just to her house to get something, I immediately start thinking, *This is crazy, it's happening too fast, my feelings are too intense.* But as soon as she's back with me I feel that sureness again, it's irresistible how badly our bodies want to be together. And we haven't even had sex yet. I can't stop staring at her, and she can't stop staring at me, we just stare at each other for hours—when we have a movie on, we have to tear our eyes away to look at the screen.

We've mostly been hanging out up here in the attic. The really crazy thing is I think Asha and Terra may be in a similar boat, anchored up in A's room. I haven't seen Ash since the Naked Party, but I've noticed her door closed and heard voices murmuring inside.…

This is what women do. We dive in. We scour each other, inspecting all of the other's treasures. We stop needing other sustenance.

I had forgotten this from when I got together with Dani, plus then we both had jobs and school. July and I don't have jobs, or responsibilities—she's gonna look for a new barbershop but for the moment all we have is this. Dani and I had sex right away, so very quickly it became about that.

July and I are trying to wait, at least a little while, so it doesn't. Instead, we've been talking about what we like. She likes to be penetrated only sometimes, she said, but she loves to strap it on.… Sometimes I lose my breath, imagining the possibilities.

I just found the list Lily and I came up with, which had I put on my altar:

<u>What I'm Looking For</u>

1. cute
2. strong
3. sweet
4. stable
5. creative
6. connection (like plugging a three-prong into an outlet, that fit, that energy)

1. Oh, yes—she has that sweet/tough combo I love, and great hair, and amazing eyes, sometimes yellow, sometimes brown…and the tattoos, I haven't even seen them all yet.…

2. Physically, yes—she can lift me! She was a swimmer in high school. But emotionally, which is what I meant here, she seems strong, self-reliant.

3. She is constantly giving me these really lovely compliments, and kissing me in these really tender places. She likes to hold my hand all the time, even in sleep. Twice she's made Sweet Adeline runs before I woke.

4. She was in therapy in N.O., seems really grounded.

5. She does visual art, collage and other stuff. And cutting hair is kind of creative too.

6. Yes, yes, yes! Perfect fit, powerful charge.

And she's funny, and silly, she makes me laugh so hard. When she's here I want my skin to be in contact with hers at all times, and when she's away I want her back immediately.

I'm already attached, and I haven't even known her a week.

Fuck.

I think I just heard the front door downstairs. Haven't told her about the journal yet. Or anything else, what happened in Japan. I will, though. I'll tell her everything, in time.

May 18

Last night July was sleeping over, and I couldn't sleep. Having someone in my bed makes it harder, I get nervous, restless. Sometimes the anxiety hits. I took some valerian and feverfew but sometimes it's hours before I fall asleep. She's the opposite—she says good night, and she's out. Maddening.

Luckily Sadie always wakes right up for me.

Sean used to tell me stories, when I couldn't sleep. He started doing it in high school, on the phone. Never said no when I asked for one, and never in 15 years told the same story twice. And they were all beautiful. I wanted him to write them down, make a book of them.

When I listened, I got excited, like a kid. *What will happen next?* The words soothed me, took me somewhere I was safe, or didn't exist at all. They helped me find a place of peace to sleep in.

I had almost forgotten how brilliant he was. How comfortable we were together. I miss that now. I'm so nervous around July, afraid she'll learn something to make her not like me.

When she snuffled in her sleep and woke up worried that I wasn't sleeping, she asked if she could do anything to help, and I asked for a story. Her hair was sticking out in front of her like a rhino horn.

July nodded, and took a couple minutes, then told me her story was about a mermaid. She knows I love the sea.

I asked, "Can her name be Freeda?"

"Yes."

"With two 'e's," I specified.

"Okay." She blinked a few times, thinking. The only light came from a candle in the alcove, and she had her eyes closed. "So Freeda, she moved to another part of the ocean. Nobody knew where she'd come from, or what she'd left behind. Some imagined a school of fish following behind her like ducklings as she left. But the truth is, she was too fast out of there for any creature to follow her."

I held my breath. Clearly July had inferred some things from the circumstances around my move.

"Soon, exploring her new neighborhood, Freeda met a male-bodied, female-brained, handsome young merman. He was always dashing hither and thither to get her attention, because once her eyes landed on him her face changed into something lighter. A face with less weight, less to hold up. The merman, his name was—"

"Sherman," I said.

"Right!" July turned on her side to face me, smiling, her eyes closing. "Sherman and Freeda liked to swim together, winding through the forests of the ocean, holding hands. He showed her all his favorite places. They would dance among the kelp, braiding their bodies in and around each other. At night, instead of looking up at the stars like we do, they looked down at the constellations of sea stars.

"So they lived harmoniously under the sea, never settling down, just roaming the underwater world together. They made friends with dolphins and rode them when they wanted to travel. They felt that the more one of them knew, the more both knew."

"And then what happened?"

"Well, they lived happily under the sea forever. They met all the glowing animals of the depths, they protected each other from the creatures with teeth, they only stopped swimming to make love now and then. And then they learned to make love as they swam, and there was nothing that could stop them."

"Ahhh, I love it. I wish that was us."

"It is us," she said. "Freeda and Sherman."

"Okay, Sherman," I said, nuzzling my head into her chest.

We fell asleep like that. It was the first time I've been able to sleep with her touching me.

May 20

July filled in some more of her backstory. We were lying in my bed after making out. Key to not going all the way is to keep our underwear on, otherwise we're just torturing ourselves. She was in a black tank top and boxers with skulls on them, and I was wearing my soft peach camisole and cotton undies with colored stars. She's delighted by all my underwear, calls the girlier ones my cupcake panties. I haven't even broken out the best ones yet—that wouldn't be fair.

The sun was going down, and I held her from behind as we watched the window turn from blue to pink to purple. She didn't have her glasses on, and I wondered how much she could see. The candles on my altar cast shadows on the eaves.

"I have something to tell you," she said.

My heart stopped, hearing that. Having my own secrets didn't make me any less afraid of hers.

"I had a brother. His name was James, but everybody called him Jamie. He was three years older than me, and we were really close.

"Jamie was a golden boy, everyone loved him. He was one of those people everyone wants to be around. So bright, so much light in him."

Like Lily, I thought.

"Like Lily," she said. "Like Lily is for you, that's what my brother was for me." I've told her how being around Lily's brightness helped me, when I arrived here.

"He was the first person I came out to. He just said, 'I know,' and gave me a big smile."

"Aw, that's sweet," I said. "He knew."

"Yeah. He was my escape from my boring-ass town

where no one understood me. I wasn't out to my parents, or any of those people, till my 20s. In high school Jamie and I went out every weekend in D.C., to bars and clubs where they didn't check ID.

"When he was 19, and I was 16, we were at a bar one night with three of his friends. He was happy that night. He was pretty much always happy.

"We were standing at the bar, and I had to go to the bathroom. I left him laughing at the bar with his friends, and I looked back and he caught my eye, like *Go ahead, I got your back.* The place wasn't that big, but it was in a rough neighborhood, and in D.C. you had to be careful.

"When I came back from the bathroom, he was lying on the floor next to the bar, his flannel shirt soaked with blood. Apparently four men in masks had come in, after fucking up a robbery out on the sidewalk, and started firing with an assault rifle. Jamie got hit, and he fell. The whole thing happened so fast, when I got back from the bathroom he was already dead."

She stopped, drew a breath. I looked over her shoulder at her face, her jaw clenched tight. "Are you okay?" I asked.

She glanced back at me and nodded. I could see she just needed to get through it.

"I stood back, watching the crowd around him grow, his screaming friends. I couldn't move. Finally one of his friends saw me and took me out to the car.

"My name was Julie, then, but everyone called me Jules," she said. "That was his name for me. So becoming July let me keep my nickname."

"He was my hero, Nara," she said, shaking. She cried for a while, then got up to use the bathroom. When she got back she lay on her back, her eyes lit by the flames. I lay on my side, holding her hand and watching her profile.

"The one good thing was that I didn't see it happen. My last memory of Jamie is him smiling and nodding at me, as I walked away."

She paused, her jaw clenching.

"My parents did not handle his death well. He was their shining son, while I was the depressive one. Without Jamie's acceptance—which was all I had, school was a total joke—I retreated into myself. My parents did the same.

"They basically forgot about me. When they did remember, it was only in reference to him. 'Why can't you get good grades, like your brother?' 'Don't you have any friends? Jamie always had such a big circle.' Why is everything so hard for you, when it was so easy for him? That's what they were essentially asking.

"It took me a long time to forgive them for that. But I worked hard at it, in my 20s. I felt like I had to get past it, because I'm all they have left. They're not perfect, but they need me."

I was surprised when I heard her say this. Because I'm all my parents have too, but I have no desire to forgive them. They don't need me, though. They only need each other.

"It took me a long time to love anything again. His friends, who were my friends too, drifted away from one another and from me once he was gone."

She said she was on Xanax for a while, for anxiety and panic attacks. And with her therapist she did EMDR, a therapy for healing from trauma. "It worked," she said. "It made it easier for me to talk about it. With other girl-friends it took me months or even years to be able to tell them. But I wanted you to know."

"Thank you. I'm really glad you told me." My heart seized with guilt and I squeezed her tighter.

May 21

I saw Lily in the kitchen this morning, for the first time since the Naked Party, and when I told her about me and July she started jumping up and down. I had to remind her to be quiet, not wake Asha.... I asked if we could borrow the station wagon so I could take July up to the Oakland hills. I wanted to show her some beauty and light after last night.

We were shy out in the world together, our first time driving together. From the driver's seat, the light on her face made new angles, more information to devour—I had to pull my eyes away from her and focus on the road. My body remembered the way, from when I used to drive over from S.F. to take Moonshine hiking in the hills.

Once we were on the trail, it all came back to me: the smell of pine, the dips and curves in the trail, they hadn't changed at all. I wanted to tell July about him, but telling her about Moony means telling her about my parents, why they don't know I'm here. That or another lie, and I didn't feel up to it after all she disclosed last night. Though not telling her felt like a lie too. I walked ahead of her on the narrow trail and swallowed my emotion.

When we reached the top, we spread our sweaty bodies out to dry in the sun. July lay on her side, looking out at the bay, propped up on an elbow, and I sat beside her, gazing out at S.F., there for the taking. I peeled us a few Cuties. We hadn't seen anyone on the way up, and it was dead quiet up there. She knew I was sad but didn't ask why. Maybe she doesn't want to have to ask.

I reached out and took her hand, massaged her palm, kissed each finger.

We were silent for a while. Then I remembered something.

I got up, excited, pulled her up and led her back down the hill, through a small opening in the trees and down to a little stream, a private spot off the path that I had discovered back in the day. It too looked the same, like no time had passed. The trees surrounding us felt like protection.

I took off my shoes and jeans and waded through the cold water in my T-shirt and underwear. Yellow lace. She hadn't seen them yet, and she smiled at them.

July rolled her jeans up and came in too, and I grabbed her tight and kissed her deeply, trying to tell her everything I couldn't say. Then I couldn't wait any longer—I unbuckled her belt, and her fly…I rinsed my tangerine-sticky fingers in the stream, and then I put my hand inside her boxers and found her clit.

I licked her ear, her neck, sucked her tongue. I was afraid to put my hand inside her, afraid she wouldn't want it, but she was so wet…I brought some of the wetness to her clit, and she moaned, her hands grabbing my ass.

I held her to me with my free arm and kissed her face, and when she opened her eyes I saw such raw desire there, I watched her open her mouth and cry out, a burst of pleasure and emotion that echoed out into the trees.

I got down to my knees in the water and held her legs and her ass, my face against her jeans, hugging her beautiful body. Stones from the stream pressed into my knees as I breathed in her rich, sharp smell…I looked up at her, and she smiled at me, such a sweet, happy smile, her hair falling over her eyes. I thought, *I love you.*

She took my hands and pulled me up, led me out of the water to a tall pine, its soft needles sticking to my feet. She pushed me gently against the tree and pulled my underwear from me and got down on her knees. Cupping my ass in her hand, protecting me from the bark, she pushed me into her mouth. She sucked me hard, and I bit my lip to keep from crying out.

I grabbed for the branches above me and moved into her, the heel of her hand cradling me, holding me up. She put her thumb inside me, and then pushed it up deeper, her fingers still holding my ass as I pressed back up against the tree. Looking up at me, she sucked on my clit as she moved her hand inside me. I looked down at her, and then my eyes fell closed.

And then I was coming too, howling up into the tree and out at the blue sky above us.

May 23

When July and I had sex up in the hills, we didn't really see each other naked. I've been feeling insecure, worried what she'd think. But today I was ready.

She led me to the foot of my bed and lay me in front of her, then took off all of my clothes, one by one, starting with my socks and ending with my bra. This time I wore black lace.

She smiled at me lying there naked, the sweetest smile, but didn't say a word. She wanted to touch me then, but I wouldn't let her. I sat up.

She stood in front of my altar, and in the light of the candles I slowly stripped her down. When I was finished, I looked at the tattoos all over her body, I looked up at her, and tears came to my eyes.

She tried to reach out to me again, but I wouldn't let her, I wanted to focus on her. I ran my hands up her legs and over her ass, reached up and along her sides, past her breasts, which are bigger than I expected, much bigger than mine, with songbirds above them.

I took her in, all of her. The animals and the skulls and the flowers, I felt like they'd been drawn there just for me. I thought, *It all had to go how it did so I would find my way here.*

And then I pulled her to my mouth, I found her clit and sucked, and she was so sweet in my mouth, like a piece of gold. I so wanted to put my hand inside her and I thought about asking her but then hesitated, afraid to do anything to fuck it up.

And then I heard her cry out for me.

She said "Nara," and in that moment I became Nara. My whole body shivered with hers as she came for me, christening me.

May 27

2:15 a.m.

Up again, can't sleep. Just before I fall asleep, I see wild and wonderful creatures and designs in white on a field of black. Once I see them I know sleep is coming, I court them, but sometimes they stay away.

I've often wished I could draw or photograph them. I tried to describe them to July yesterday.

"That's the hypnagogic state," she said. "The limbo between consciousness and sleep." I'm always learning stuff like this from her. She has ten years on me, plus we have such different interests.

She told me she's worked with this state, a kind pf precursor to lucid dreaming. "You lie down with your arm up, and when you start to fall asleep your arm will fall, waking you to whatever you had seen or felt in that moment. You can ask your subconscious for help."

"Subconscious, help me figure out what to do about Jules. I'm falling in love with her."

It just popped out. We froze.

"She loves you too," she said in the deep voice of my subconscious.

And then we kissed. And moved into the hypnotic agog state—another thing entirely.

May 28

Every time we have sex our bodies create something new. We're changing together, getting deeper every day, so it's different every time, we're different.

Her skin so soft on mine…just that is so, so sweet, so soothing, I never want her to leave, we can move together for hours, pressing up against each other, holding on to each other for dear life.

I told her I don't like having my nipples sucked, because I'm afraid there's still milk in them. It's torture, though, all I want is her mouth on them.

Sometimes she pulls my hair back, holds my arms down, gentle but firm. The other day, I got one arm free, and put my hand at her opening, looking into her eyes until they softened in acquiescence. She let me.

And then I was inside her, moaning from the feeling, lost in it, her wetness easing my hand almost all the way in…. I found her clit with my thumb, moved my hand in and out, so turned on by her wetness and sounds of submission that I had to remind myself to focus on her clit… and then it was all over. Fast like always.

She came, and came, and came, bucking against me, giving in to the pleasure more completely than ever before.

After she came I moved my body along the length of hers and kissed her, holding her head and finding places for my lips in her neck. She came down quivering and holding me tight. I shook her to her core, and she let me.

Every time we get deeper. Every time she makes me forget everything and give myself over. I offer myself to her, like a gift.

I've been getting to know her toys, which she brought over. With Dani I had rejected dildos as what I was trying to leave behind. The way she wanted to do it, so aggressive, like a guy—I never trusted her enough, I guess. Now I know what I missed.

When July straps it on, it's really like an extension of her. Like an ultimate expression, not a costume. She takes it seriously but does it casually, and it makes sense. And it feels so damn good to be taken like that.

It's like my brain shuts off and all I can do is feel. Finally! I needed a break from all that thinking.

The sex seals us, keeps us close, the shared memory of the ecstasy of our skin. We sleep naked, and sometimes in the middle of the night our bodies start up on their own, rocking against each other like tectonic plates.

"That was one of my top five orgasms ever," I told her the other day. She no longer believes me when I say it was my best, so I've become more discerning. "That hella tingly kind when you just touch my clit…like all my nerves are on fire. And then the orgasm feels like it lasts forever…I could keep going, and going…. One of these days you'll push me over the edge and end up with a vegetable for a girlfriend."

"Mmm, an ear of corn, I'd nibble all your kernels off."

"Organic, of course."

"Of course. No Monsanto. Not sexy."

June 1

We all hung out in the backyard today—it was perfect weather, sunny but not too hot. I lay on the couch with my head in July's lap, as Terra consulted with Asha on the veggies and Lily watered with the gray water.

July drank her beer, amused. "Wow, NorCal," she said. "Like another species."

"I like to call them hippunks. Not totally hippie, not totally punk, but in between."

"Should we go have some corn on the cob?" she asked, looking down at me. Our new euphemism for getting busy. My red gingham sheets do look like a tablecloth.

So we excused ourselves and went up to the attic for a little picnic.

Later I went over to July's house and she answered the door with one blood-red eye.

"I got tea tree in my eye," she said.

"That's a pretty hippie problem to have," I said. I like to tease her about being a hippie.

"Hey, you're the one with an herb closet," she said.

I met July's roommate—her ex-girlfriend Lexy. She's this kind of high-femme, bossy type. Maybe she still wants July and that's why she was bitchy to me?

She's lived next door for a while and seems a little territorial. She asked me what I thought of the block and I said I wasn't thrilled about the crack house.

She said, "Oh, them, they're cool."

"You're friends with them?"

"We look out for each other."

"It's just that they're out there talking shit *all day*. And I can hear every word from my room. It gets old."

"That's just Oakland. You'll get used to it."

I just stood looking at her, holding my ground as July watched us, looking amused. Finally she offered to show me around.

Their house is newer than ours, just a basic house. And there's this heavy energy over there. It must be Lexy, since July just moved in.

But of course July wanted me to like it, and I did like her room. She's covered her ceiling in images of the ocean, so that when you lie on her bed it looks like the sea on her ceiling. She said she culled her decades of *National Geographic*s before she left and brought the ocean pics with her.

Although it is super convenient having her live next door, I don't feel at all good about this Lexy thing. July says not to worry, that they weren't together very long and it was a long time ago. That Lexy is a top and that was one of their problems.

More information than I needed, J. Thanks.

June 6

It took me a long time to come today. The old nervousness is back, and it's keeping me from relaxing. So annoying. My past breathing fire into my new now, everything tinged with soot.

But I was desperate for the release, so I didn't tell her to stop, even though she must have wanted to. She always comes in like five minutes.

It finally came, and it was worth waiting for.

I so want to let go of everything I've been holding so tight, just let it tumble out. Sometimes I think she could take it all.

I always stop short before I say anything, though. Too afraid. I give her my body instead, all of me, every cell.

It has to be enough. And for now, it is. We made a bed fort, pinned a sheet to the edge of the eave, so it's just the bed and altar inside. I'm in here now writing, candle glowing like a lantern in a tent. When we're in here, it's more than enough. So we just try to come often, and stay as long as we can.

It's like being a kid again. We made our own little world and everything else has to stay out. Though I have to say, I feel bad but all day I was wanting her to leave so I could write in here. I haven't told her about the journal yet. I'm too afraid she'll want to read it.

Sometimes, lately—don't tell me the honeymoon is already over—she's too much. It's too intense. And she can see it in my face. And then we have to process it…. Being a lesbian is annoying sometimes.

Anyway she finally left to take a shower at her place and I got stoned in the fort. I don't get high when she's around since she's not into it. She doesn't mind if I do but that just makes me feel self-conscious, like eating in front of someone who's not eating.

June 13

5:10 a.m.
Woke up early again, couldn't get back to sleep. I'm writing in the fort, at the foot of the bed.

July is asleep, like a kid without her glasses on. I wonder what she was like—I know she wore hand-me-downs from her brother. The other day she showed me a photo of them. She was 3, chubby and happy in shorts and a T-shirt, looking up at him. He was 6, and wearing overalls. Smiling at the camera, holding her hand.

Little Jules and James.

It made me cry. How wonderful to have a sibling, and how terrible to have him taken away.

I still haven't told her my birth name, and she hasn't asked. She can look me up online, then, and there's not much there but I'd feel too exposed. If I'm honest, anything outside the fort feels too exposed.

Something's coming, I can feel it. Something not good.

June 16

Ingy turned 14! We convinced Claudia to let her have a costume party in the backyard. July hooked up a sound system, and Ingy made a mix of her favorite songs. It was a beautiful sunny day, after a week of gray. July grilled veggie burgers and dogs, and Asha and Terra made kabobs downstairs in Claudia's kitchen. I made potato salad, Japanese style, with carrots and cucumbers, and Lily made a yummy vegan mac and cheese. Claudia brought several pizzas and a bunch of pastries from Arizmendi.

Ingy's costume was gruesome—white face paint with blood dripping down, ripped black tights and cutoffs and her hair all wild, very Pauline in *Heavenly Creatures*. It gave me the shivers, especially since Pauline kills her mom in that movie.

I wonder why more teens don't kill their parents. It's such a heavy time, all those emotions and hormones, and parents are the perfect scapegoat, if not directly responsible for our angst. Luckily Ingy has us to vent to when they fight. She runs upstairs, instead of away.

Claudia has been a rock for all of us at one time or another. Even July the other day went out to smoke and ended up chatting with Claudia on the backyard couch for hours. I watched them from the attic window, wondering if they were talking about me.

Claudia's our matriarch. So on Ingy's birthday we assured her that we would take care of everything, and all she had to do was make a spectacular cake.

Oh, and get their home ready for a dog. I told her about Sharky, and a couple days ago she and I went to the shelter and he was still there, looking like he couldn't care less whether we sprung him or left him there for eternity. Claudia was amused, had been expecting some cuddly puppy and instead here was this scruffy mutt, the least needy of the bunch. So Claudia adopted him in her daughter's name, and we took him to Brix's, where they've been taking care of him till today.

Ingy's friends filed in like the walking dead. Other than a sexy Dorothy (Sharky would make a good Toto when he arrived) and a mouse, it was zombies and skeletons and vampires, oh my. The adults, on the other hand, were too wholesome: I was a clown, Lily a frog, Asha and Terra cats. July was wearing those glittery alien antennae from the '80s. Claudia was a witch—she decided she might as well lean into it. Her cake was red velvet on the inside and black and white on the outside, pomegranate blood dripping sexily down all around. It was upstairs in our fridge, all of our food on the counter making room for the three-layer concoction.

Ingy buzzed around her friends, a dozen or so of them sprawled across the couch and on the lawn, eating and chatting. Mostly too cool to dance, though Ingy's mix rocked. She seemed confident with them, in her element.

Asha and Terra cuddled on a big armchair, sharing a plate of food. Sometimes it's a bit much. The lack of separation between where one starts and the other stops—like they want to become one person. The other day they went to the *DMV* together. Terra had to go to deal with her van registration, and Asha *went with her.*

And I know July wishes we were more like them. As if being next-door neighbors isn't enough.

I heard a bark. Sharky! Lily and Brix had brought him over, and he came coolly strolling into the party, sniffing around, a hilarious big pink bow around his neck. Ingy saw him, and looked over at me with excitement. I smiled and nodded. Then she looked at her mom, who also smiled and nodded, and she ran over to Claudia and knocked her over with a giant hug.

Then she ran over to Sharky and started petting him, crying to her friends, "I got a dog, I got a dog!" She called over to me, "What's his name again, Nara?"

"Sharky," I called back.

"Oh, yeah!" she said, cracking up. "Sharky!"

Sharky knew his name, and looked up casually every time we said it.

"He's the coolest! Right?" We all agreed.

June 18

July got a job! I met her there today while she was working. It's a fancy new barbershop that already has lines out the door, spilling out onto this charming alley that's closed to cars. There's also a custom-filled doughnut shop and a boutique selling succulents and handmade pots. July draped her geisha proudly around the gorgeous old black-and-white barber chair at her station.

At her last shop in the French Quarter, she said, the shop's older, dapper African-American clients dismissed her at first, thinking there was no way a white woman could do them up like the owner, himself an older Black man. But they trusted him, and one by one they gave her a chance. After a while, she said, butch dykes started coming in.

Alley Cuts is more hipster than old-school, but I think July feels comfortable there. There's a tattoo place around the corner, and she's gone in to chat with the artists.

It's good to see her feeling fulfilled. We have less time together now, but that may be a good thing. She keeps worrying we won't have any time together once I start school in the fall. I figure in a month I'll just tell everyone that I've decided to put school off for a while. And then I'll start looking for a job. If I were to look now it would be weird, since they all think I'm starting school soon.

Lily and I rode our bikes to People's Park today, for a music festival. We lay in the grass and drank Terra's home-brewed beer. Lily's last semester of school is this fall, then she wants to find a job as a pediatric nurse in a clinic. I felt nervous when she spoke about school, worried she would ask about my program, but she didn't.

I was planning to ask her help in finding work, but I suddenly couldn't imagine being out in the world and public again. Nothing sounds right. I'm not ready.

There were tons of kids at the festival, dancing and chasing each other around. Wild and free.

My mind flashed to Kai's face, suddenly—tiny Kai-Kai, my only two-year-old student. His eyes were full of fear as my powder-blue school slippers turned black with blood. A memory I didn't even know I had.

Just one horror-movie strobe-light flash, and he was gone.

Lily was saying that she's accepted that she may not be having a baby from her own body, but she thinks maybe a baby will come to her, somehow.

What happened to those slippers? What happened to those kids?

July has asked if I want them. Kids, not slippers. I think she's getting a little tired of me changing the subject.

June 20

I woke this morning to harmonica floating into the attic. Irritated because it was 6:15 but curious why Brix was out there so early. Then I remembered he and Lily were going away on a big bike trip, so I pulled on a sweater and went down to say bye. July was sleeping at her place.

Lily was in the kitchen making food for their trip. She looked so happy, organizing their food and packing it into their giant packs with care. She was quiet, but gave me a big hug.

"When are you guys leaving?" I asked as I put the kettle on.

"As soon as these granola bars are done."

"How long will you be gone?"

"Two weeks. Brix's birthday is tomorrow. We're going to drive all day today so we can be in Zion tomorrow."

"Nice. Isn't yours coming up too?"

"July 23."

On the anarchist calendar in the kitchen, I drew a heart with an L in the middle of July 23, noting that the Egyptian Revolution started on July 23, 1952. I poured the water into a pot of my good green tea, poured a cup for Lily, carried two cups and the teapot to the porch.

"Hey, dude," I said as I sat on the porch seat, poured Brix some tea.

"Hey," he said. "Thanks."

"Your harmonica's sweet to wake up to." I pulled my knees to my chest and pulled my sweater over them, against the early morning cold. Brix was wearing a red cardigan of Lily's over one of his KALX T-shirts. When Bogus Basin played on the Cal Berkeley station, the DJ let him and Merry pick out a few shirts. The station is on nonstop in our house, like a soundtrack.

"Oh, shit. Sorry I woke you."

"It's cool. I'm glad I can wish you bon voyage. You excited?"

"Yeah, it's been too long. Zion is like home away from home. I used to go there all the time in high school."

"How'd you end up here, anyway?" I asked him.

"Merry came here first and I came to stay with her, play some shows, then I started fixing bikes and just never left. Being in the city makes me crazy sometimes, though. I'm lucky Lil needs to get away too."

We smiled at each other. It's easy being with him. I called in to Lily, "Need help with anything?"

"No, I'm good," she called back.

I heard Asha's door pop open, and she came sleepily around the corner, into the kitchen. "What are you freaks yelling about?" she said, falling against Lily and snuggling her head against her shoulder.

Lily brought some pieces of granola bar out to the porch and said, "Tell me what you think."

"Mmm," Asha said, following her.

Lily looked at Brix like she was giving him one last chance to back out. "You ready?"

His eyes locked on hers. "Ready when you are."

"Can we help load the car?" I asked.

"Speak for yourself," Asha muttered.

"Nope, we only have one bag each," Lily said. "We have to strap everything to the bikes." She packed the bars in her backpack.

As they put their shoes and jackets on, Asha sleepily half-hugged, half-hung on me. "The whole place to ourselves," she said.

As they headed down the stairs, big packs bumping the

ceiling of the steep staircase, I remembered following Lily up those stairs just five months ago.

We followed them down and hugged goodbye on the porch.

"Farewell," Asha said.

"Be safe," I said, and gave them both a kiss on the cheek.

We watched from the porch as they climbed into the wagon after tossing their packs in the back. The bikes were already on top.

We waved as they drove off, beeping once as they turned the corner. Then we came back up and fell on the couch and I asked what's happening with her and Terra. Turns out they're in pretty much exactly the same boat as me and July—the love boat.

I asked how the sex is, and she just nodded, big eyes bright. She just kept nodding.

"Is she here?"

"Yeah, sleeping. Is July?"

"No, she's at her place. Maybe I better go over and wake her up."

"Yeah. You can bring her a granola bar."

"Get some sleep," I said, pushing Asha into her room and heading into the kitchen to bundle up a couple of the bars Lily had left for us.

I went out back, climbed over the fence, then boosted myself up into July's window and climbed into her bed. I put my arms around her, and she grunted but didn't wake up. Then, miraculously, I fell into an easy sleep.

SUMMER

June 21

I went to the Derby farmers market today, to celebrate that it's summer. When I got back, the sun was setting, and Sean's brother Patrick was sitting on the stoop.

No one was home. Patrick was impeccably dressed, more intimidating than ever.

I started to retreat back out the gate. He laughed and said, "Oh, no you don't," and grabbed my produce bag from my shoulder. "Come over here and talk to me," he said, nodding toward the porch.

I was scared. I felt like a little kid about to be punished. I sat down on the steps, but he stayed standing.

"What the fuck are you doing here? What is this place?" The next-door neighbors stared with interest from their porch. I looked nervously toward July's place.

"It's a house," I said lamely.

"Why are you here?"

"This is where I came." A calm came over me. *I only have to answer his questions.*

"Why haven't you told Sean where you are?" he asked.

"I wasn't ready."

"Do you have any idea what you put him through? He's a wreck, Sara. So worried about you."

He was waiting for an answer, but I didn't have one. I was mentally calculating the time, realizing I didn't know July's schedule, she could get home at any moment.

But instead, just then Ingy came home. The gate slammed behind her, and she just stood there looking at Patrick, this big huge man glaring at her.

She looked up at me. "It's okay," I told her, and she walked up the steps, then into her place, and locked the door.

"You just started a whole new life so you wouldn't have to deal with the old one? Is she your new kid?"

I saw Ingy looking through the front window at us and knew she could hear him. She looked scared.

There was a terrible dread in my stomach. "I'm sorry, Patrick, I know it's hard to understand. But I just couldn't deal. I had to leave."

"You're such a chickenshit, Sara," he said. "Jesus."

"I know. I'm sorry. Will you tell Sean I'm sorry?" My voice broke.

"Fucking tell him yourself!" His voice rose and he clenched his fists. The neighbors were enjoying the drama.

I had a flash of understanding, in that moment. This is unbelievable to me now, but it was the first time I realized that Sean is grieving too. I'm so selfish, I never even thought about how he lost Willow too.

I made myself stop crying, shook my head. "I'll get in touch with him, Patrick. Okay? I'll tell him where I am."

"You fucking better. Or I will."

And then Asha walked through the gate.

For a second all I could think was, *It happened. It's happening.* My worlds finally collided. I felt suspended again, between here and there. My head suddenly empty as a cloud.

"Nara. You okay?"

I suddenly saw how lucky the women at the shelter are, how good she must be at her job. That fierceness.

"Nara?" Patrick said, laughing now. "*Nara?* Fucking perfect."

Patrick had hated Sean being in Japan and he blamed me. It was true, that was one of the reasons Sean had wanted to move so far away—because his relationship with his brother had felt difficult once he and I got together. Patrick hadn't liked us as a couple. Maybe he knew I would end up hurting Sean.

Patrick stood glaring at me, his large frame not fitting under the overhang of the porch, and I moved one step up, away from him.

Asha stopped halfway up the stairs, assessing the situation. She scanned his preppy outfit, football-player frame, angry eyes. Ingy peeked through the curtain, and Asha saw her, and the neighbors gawking.

She looked at me, and finally her eyes rested on Patrick.

"Time for you to go," she said.

He laughed again. "You better ask 'Nara' who she really is."

"Go," she said again, and the threat in her voice got his attention.

"I'll go, but Sara, I'm giving you a week, and if you don't get in touch with Sean, I'll bring him back with me."

I nodded. He turned away and didn't look back, the gate slamming behind him.

Ingy opened their front door and came out to the porch.

"I'm sorry, you guys, that was crazy." I looked at the two of them.

"Who the hell is he?" Asha asked.

I looked over at Ingy, who still looked scared.

"Nara," Asha said. "Or is it Sara? Who was that?"

I wanted to lie. I knew if I told her I'd have to tell Lily too, and July.

It was only ever a house of cards, I realized. *Not a home.*

They were waiting, and there was no way out. I said, "He's my ex-boyfriend's brother."

"Okay," Asha said. "What is he doing here?"

They were both still standing, looking down at me.

Like all the trust I'd built with them was gone.

"He's angry because I left his brother and didn't tell him where I was going."

"When was this?" Asha asked.

"When I came here," I said.

"Hmm," she said. "You never mentioned that."

"I know," I said. "It's a long story."

"I'm sure it is," Asha said. "Maybe one day you'll tell us." She looked at Ingy then, and something passed between them, some mutual disappointment. "You okay?" Asha asked Ingy, and she nodded. "Let's get you started on your homework." The two of them went into Ingy's place, leaving me sitting on the porch alone.

The neighbors were chatting and laughing like nothing had happened.

June 23

Dear Sean,

Your big brother is making me email you. We had a nice little visit yesterday. How the fuck did he find me, anyway? Why does he hate me so much?

Dear Sean,

Why did you convince me that we should have a baby? Did you really think it could save us?

Dear Sean,

Why were you not there for me, when I needed you? Why were you not ever there?

Dear Sean,

I'm ashamed of what I did, leaving you. I know it seems psychotic. It was. I was crazy.

Dear Sean,

How can I apologize for what I've done? How could I just leave you like that, and hide from you all this time, after all we've been through? How could I do that to you?

Dear Sean,

I couldn't go back to that classroom. I couldn't live in that apartment, hearing the kids above me. The failure, and the pain. I couldn't deal with it for even one day.
    You weren't there. You didn't see.

Dear Sean,

I'm sorry I hurt you. There's a lot more to say, but that's where I'll start.

If you want to be in touch, please write me back or call me.

Love,

Sara
510-555-2317

June 24

July and I got in our first fight today.

We were sitting on the back porch drinking gin and tonics and she asked about my place in Japan. What was it like? Did I live by myself?

"Why are you asking me this now?" I was afraid Asha might have told her what happened the other day. She had told me she wouldn't, that she would let me tell July, Claudia, and Lily myself.

"I've been asking all along, Nara. I want to know more about you."

Something shifted in me then. Suddenly it seemed ridiculous, the amount of energy I've spent hiding such stupid shit.

I said, "My apartment was very nice. Very modern. I had an awesome tub, with special jets. There was a walking path in front of my place that led to the beach. In the summer it's warm at night and there are food and drink tents, you can get noodles and a beer. Watch the sunset. Make a fire. Or swim. I swam a lot there."

She watched me, surprised. "Did you live by yourself?"

"No, I had a boyfriend. But he wasn't around much."

"Ah. Where was he?"

"Traveling for work."

"Why is it so hard to get information out of you?"

I paused, then said, "There's stuff I can't talk about." It was the first time I admitted that I'm not telling her everything, and she pounced on it.

"You can tell me! Baby, you can trust me."

"I do trust you. I just need you to trust me. I will tell you everything in time. I really want to. I just need you to be patient."

Her eyes filled with hurt and frustration, behind her glasses. "I told you about my brother. That wasn't easy for me."

"I know. And I'm so glad you did."

"So why can't you fucking do the same? Is your pain is more special than ours?"

I froze at that, felt myself harden. I couldn't stand sitting there with her anymore. I got up and went down the back stairs and around the side of the house, where I'd left my bike.

She called down to me from the porch, "Nara, don't leave."

But I was out of there. I rode around for hours, almost getting lost in the industrial streets of West Oakland.

The sun started going down, and I headed back, but when I got there I slowly circled the house. If July was still at my house, I decided I would just tell her that I was too tired to fight, and it would be true.

But she wasn't here. And she hasn't texted.

June 26

July and I were planning to go to the Dyke March in the Mission today, so she got the day off. But we were still kind of raw from our fight the other night, even though we made up yesterday. As we were about to head to BART with Asha and Terra, I asked July if she really wanted to go, and she shook her head no. We needed to be alone, we needed something to put us back together again.

So we decided to go to Santa Cruz. We borrowed Lexy's car and July drove, windows down and singing the Smiths, looking like Morrissey with her pompadour. I started to cry, so relieved we were back in love again, and had to wipe away the tears under my sunglasses. It felt like we might die at any moment, speeding up and around that narrow mountain road, but it would indeed have been a pleasure and a privilege to die by her side, singing and crying and blowing in the sunshine.

We rode the rickety old Giant Dipper first. We chatted with the boy standing in front of us in line, a small 10-year-old with dark hair and dark eyes, riding by himself. July was good with him, asking him questions, making him laugh. It seemed to come easily to her, whereas I was all nervous.

After a while, though, he brought a little of my ease with kids out in me. It was a long line.

I wondered what kind of parents we'd make, July and I, what kind of kid we'd make. It was the first time I let myself imagine it.

When it was finally our turn, he got in the front car, and on the first long climb he turned around and found us a few cars back and waved. We waved back, holding hands. Then we crested, and hurtled downward, and I closed my eyes and screamed through the rest.

When we came out and looked at the picture of us, I saw the boy in the front car, arms up, face lit with fear or joy. He reminded me of someone. I couldn't take my eyes off him. Then the picture flashed away, and he was gone.

July chased me down to the ocean. I lifted my skirt and was tying it up in a knot when she pushed me down in the water. We rolled around in the shallows, splashing and dunking each other. She can make me laugh so hard, like when I was a kid, where I stop making any sound and just shake.

We got out and lay on our towels. She put her Ray-Bans on, her hair floating back like a wave. I kissed her on the cheek, then turned over on my belly for a nap, reaching behind me for her hand, which she let me take. The sun dried my clothes as I slept.

Later we rode the Cliff Hanger. You lie on your belly, and the ride lifts you into the air, up and around like you're flying. I looked over at July and she was laughing hysterically. It felt amazing up there, the wind and the sun and our love. I closed my eyes and imagined I was a pelican, skimming the water, up and away from all of it.

When I opened my eyes I saw the boy from the roller coaster, standing in line for the ride. He was watching me, but I couldn't read his face. I turned my head to watch him as we sped past, and as the boy faded from view into my mind slid a memory of Sean at that age. The same soulful almond eyes and sweet round face.

When we rounded the corner again, the boy was gone.

In the leaving, the forgetting, I'd almost forgotten what he looks like. I had to forget his beauty in order to leave him.

I haven't heard back from him.

June 27

Terra moved in! She was weeding when I went down to water the veggies tonight. We shared a joint on the couch when we were done.

"Asha is driving me crazy," she said.

"I hear you," I said. "July, not Asha."

"Women—can't live with 'em, but they're better than men."

I snorted. "So true."

"She's taking a nap." She offered me a tall brown bottle of beer. "I started this batch at my old place, and it's finally ready."

I took a sip. It was dark, bitter in a good way. It felt intimate, sharing it with her. Sitting on the couch with Terra, I realized how cloistered we've all been.

"Cheers. Welcome to the house." I took a celebratory swig and handed it back. "What's up with Asha?" I figured maybe I could help, and that it would be good to hear what's going on with Asha, since she's not talking to me. Ever since the Patrick thing, she's been avoiding me. I don't know what to say to her.

Terra passed me the joint, then pulled a cigarette out of her pocket and lit it. "We're just so different."

"Really? It seems like you're into the same things…or is everyone around here into herbs and biodiesel?" Terra runs biodiesel in her camper van. I swapped her the joint for the cigarette.

"No, that's true…I guess I mean personality-wise. For one thing, she *hates* to process. I need to talk, to work through stuff. But she hates it."

"Bad lesbian."

"Ha! I know!" She laughed.

"You know what, though, I'm like that too. July freaking *loves* to process. But it's a total downer for me."

"But that's how things get better! By talking about them."

"I feel like things get better when behaviors change. I would rather use that energy to actually try and get better as humans. Talking about it only makes it worse, for me."

"Oh, interesting. You are totally like Asha in that way. This is good."

"Yeah, and you're like July. She says I'm like a guy— always wanting to fuck, never to talk." Terra laughed.

I stretched my body back over the side of the couch, looked up at the few stars. "I wish we could turn out all the lights, so we could see the stars."

"I know." She stretched her slender torso back and looked up too. "I lived in Joshua Tree for a while, in the van, and the stars were crazy there." She passed me the beer, and I finished it and set the bottle on the grass.

"We should all go camping, or something," I said. "Do you two have any breaks coming up?"

"I have the whole summer off." She's studying landscape architecture. "I can always skip out on my Spiral Garden volunteering."

"Okay, I'll see what July's schedule is like. Wanna go in?" I asked, handing her the bottle.

"Yeah, I'm hungry."

"We got our CSA today, I was gonna stir-fry some veggies. We could make muffins."

"That'll get Asha up." She headed up the back stairs, and I followed. "Thanks for listening."

As she disappeared into Asha's room, I plopped on the couch and picked up an herb catalog and looked through it, too lazy to get up and find something else to read. Then I started hearing sex sounds from Asha's room, right behind my head. I turned on some Nina Simone, to give them a little privacy, went into the kitchen and started scheming.

Cooking high is fun, I get creative and stop worrying about things turning out perfectly. But I can't follow a recipe for shit.

Come save me from myself, I called to them telepathically. But they need their sex. Just like July and I do. Like medicine.

June 28

Asha brought up the Patrick thing last night. I ended up making the stir-fry and muffins by myself, and then July came over and Asha and Terra came out and we all ate together. We made plans to go to Portland this weekend, it's Asha's birthday on Sunday.

I figured if Asha wanted to go on a road trip with me we must be cool. But then I went out to the porch bench to smoke and she followed me out.

Quietly, she said, "I've been thinking about what that guy said. That you're pretending to be someone you're not. It is of course a tad disturbing." She took off her glasses and cleaned them on her shirt. "Does July know?"

I shook my head. I was still pretty stoned, and I froze up. Playing dead.

"You need to tell her. It's not fair to lie to her."

I nodded.

"I can't believe I used to feel so close to you."

And I looked up at her and saw her sad eyes, and remembered how close I had felt to her too. I was thinking about how to start, what I could say, and then Terra came out looking for Asha. I could tell she felt the tension between Asha and me, and I wondered if Asha had told her anything.

They went back inside and I went down to the yard and lay down on the couch, watched the stars for a while. I felt like it was them against me—my roommates, July, Sean and Patrick.

Finally I went around front, used the spare key, to avoid them hanging out in the living room. I went up to my room and got under the covers in the dark. By the time July found me, I was asleep.

It's too late to tell her. She'll leave me if she knows the truth.

June 29

I just got off the phone with Sean. He finally called. We talked for four and a half hours. He said he doesn't know if he can forgive me. If he even wants to try.

He gave me the silent treatment for about half of it. But I could hear him breathing on the other end, so I just kept filling in the space, apologizing, trying to explain. How he wouldn't have let me go. How I needed to go.

When he finally started talking, he sounded terrible. All the life was gone from his voice.

He said, "I couldn't believe you would just leave me like that. I still can't believe it, actually, that you wouldn't want to go through it together. I didn't understand what happened. I was worried about you, at first, and then I got angry. I hated you. I hated whatever you'd become."

Nara. He hated Nara, I told myself. *Not me.* At the time I took comfort in that, but now it seems like dissociation. Nara *is* me. Isn't she?

"But you're right, I wouldn't have let you leave so soon after you lost the baby. You probably didn't even see a doctor after the miscarriage, did you? Never mind, don't answer that.

"Because you know what? If you want to be irresponsible, that's not on me. You removed me from the equation. After a while I didn't have the energy to hate you anymore. I was worried, though. I kept thinking you'd come back. I had to be there in case you came back. In case you needed me."

He started to cry and my ears started ringing. My chest turned cold.

"Why couldn't you have just gone somewhere else in Japan, stayed in a hotel until I got back?"

I knew that I had to answer him, but I was totally frozen. Short-circuited.

Finally I forced open my mouth and made myself speak. My voice was dull, completely lacking emotion. "I had to forget it to survive it. So I couldn't be around you. Because you'll always remind me of her."

"Since you weren't there," he said, energy coming back into his voice, "it *was* like nothing happened. I felt like I was going crazy. Had I lost my mind and imagined the whole thing?"

And it was so overwhelmingly reassuring, having someone who understood, the cold in me melted spontaneously. I told him how many times these past months I've thought the same thing, that I might have lost my mind, that maybe it was all just a bad dream.

He hasn't been writing. He's never not written, since high school, he's always been working on something.

We cried a lot. The first time I said her name, it was the first time I had said it out loud since I lost her—as soon as I said *Willow* we both started to sob, like it was contagious. It was an overwhelming relief to talk to the only other person who knew how it felt. To be able to talk about her, and to know we're not crazy. It was painful, and terrible, but now I feel like I can breathe again for the first time since I left Japan. Like a real person.

I didn't tell him about July. I didn't have the heart to.

Neither of us mentioned my seeing Patrick. Sean might be mad at him for coming here.

Sean is living with Patrick in Echo Park. He has a bunch of my stuff down there, he said, stuff I left behind that he thought I'd want, and my last check, and a box of drawings the kids made for me after I left.

I didn't ask him how Haruka reacted to my leaving. I

didn't want to know. I asked him to mail the check but to hold on to the rest. So he has my address now.

I told him he can still call me Sara. It's surprising, but it didn't bother me to hear it like I thought it would. It almost sounds pretty to me now.

It's so silly, how scared I was of this person who loves me so much. He will forgive me, he has to. As awful as it was for me to leave him in Kamakura, I knew he would forgive me, or I wouldn't have been able to do it.

We'll be okay again, eventually. We have too much history not to be.

July 1

Sean and I have been texting a little these past few days, and today I called him again. I probably won't be able to text or call from Portland, and there was so much more I wanted to say, to ask.

I told him I've been writing a journal. He said he had an idea for a short story. When I asked what it's about, he said, "Some bitch who leaves her boyfriend behind in Japan." I told him that's what I've been writing about too.

I'm ashamed of my childishness, in leaving him. I ran, like I always do.

He said he looked for me in Nara. He knew how badly I wanted to go there, so a month after I left he flew to Nara and stayed there for a week, going to the Nara Daibutsu every day and hoping to see me there. When he didn't, he said, he prayed, for the first time in his life. He sat with the Nara Daibutsu all day and prayed, just like I had with the Kamakura Daibutsu.

He said it was like a dream, with the deer everywhere and a mist covering the city. I wanted to tell him about my dream of Nara, but I couldn't, I was crying so hard, imagining him there, the pain he must have been in. He said he's glad he went, because the Nara Daibutsu gave him strength to do what he had to do, to move away from our beautiful place that had turned toxic.

So that's why Patrick was so angry when he heard I'd named myself Nara.

He said he had told Patrick we were in touch, and Patrick told him he had come here. He told me how Patrick found me.

He was staying with his and Sean's childhood friend George, and saw me in Walgreens. He followed me out, and now that I remember I actually saw him, the flash of his big body moving in and then out of my peripheral vision. He hid behind one of the big pillars out front, then jotted down Lily's license plate number as I drove away. He gave the plate number to his dad's client the cop, who got him our address, and he drove straight here.

Sean asked if I was seeing anyone, so I told him about July. I didn't get into detail, just told him the basics. It felt terrible—I don't think he's interested in me now, after what I did, but it had to hurt—but also really good to be honest with him.

I didn't ask if he'd met anyone. I didn't want to know, and I felt like he deserved some privacy. What right do I have to know about his love life?

I wanted to tell him about the New Year's Eve party, but I couldn't do it. I don't want him to blame me, to hate me again. But also, I don't want him to have those pictures in his mind like I do. I want him to imagine Willow just swimming away peacefully, just not meant to be.

July 3

Tonight July and I celebrated that it's her month. She'd told me her favorite movie is *Hedwig and the Angry Inch*, so I rented it for us, and got takeout Thai food. Everyone was out, for once, so we had the house to ourselves. Lily and Brix are still on their trip.

We ate a pot truffle and drank champagne with raspberries while we watched *Hedwig*. I'd never seen it before, and I loved it. July sang along, jumping up on the coffee table for "The Origin of Love." She's a total rock star!

I was so happy. It was the truffle and the champagne and the relief of being in touch with Sean again, but really it was her. When I looked up at her on the coffee table above me, singing into her champagne glass like a microphone, not taking her eyes off me for a second, the incredible animation dancing behind her on the screen…it was art and love and sex and music all mashed up together, and I felt so lucky.

I can't lose her. It isn't an option.

After the movie we were wired, so we decided to ride our bikes over to Art Murmur. On the first Friday of every month, a bunch of art galleries in Oakland stay open late, a few blocks near downtown are closed to traffic, and Oakland comes out to play.

On the street tonight it suddenly occurred to me that I don't have to worry about Sean finding me anymore. I felt an exhilarating freedom, walking in the middle of the street, a wildness in my limbs. I grabbed July's hand and realized that it was our first time on the street like that, relaxed and together like a real couple. I kissed her, long and deep, an apology and a promise.

The art was cool, and so was this dance party that broke

out in the middle of Telegraph. I pulled July into the middle of the throng and then lost myself to the drums, almost forgetting where I was until I opened my eyes.

The anarchists and the hipsters and the oldies, all their heads bobbing together in the dark. I nestled my back into July and held onto her arms around me, safe in the swarm.

Down the street, I saw the red neon of the Fox Theater pulsing OAKLAND, OAKLAND, OAKLAND. The sign I had seen above Daibutsu, telling me to come here.

I heard him telling me, *You did it, kid. You made it.*

July 5

9:07 a.m.
Portland, Oregon
"Joni Mitchell makes me want to do meth!" July yelled over the wind. Or that's what I thought she said. I was lying in her lap in the back seat and I started laughing and couldn't stop, and then she was too. Every time we got close to calming down, Joni's earnest voice cracked us up all over again. I rolled into July, laughed into her, our bodies shaking together.

We were in the car with Asha and Terra all day yesterday and it was clearly making us crazy. Asha's biodiesel Jetta made it over the mountains and into a gorgeous gay sunset. We left the windows down in the back seat, bonding over all the ways we were different from our friends in the front.

July seems to enjoy the us against them feeling—not in any kind of competitive way, though maybe a subtle superiority. She *is* more than a decade older than they are. And the things at which they excel are things July is disinterested in. The planning and preparing of food, for example. They both have yeast infections, so they made candida-free food—for the whole trip. How lesbian can you be? When we stopped at the biodiesel station to fill up, they had to get everything out and spent literally an hour eating, while July and I ate our sandwiches in five minutes.

Two whirlwind romances unfolding side by side, like some kind of race. It's hard not to feel competitive.

It wasn't easy to get Asha to agree to the trip. She's so fussy about sleep, she never wants to go away. We needed her to say yes because we wanted her to drive. Finally Terra threatened that if she wouldn't go to Portland we would take her camping instead.

"Anything but that," Asha said, waving her hands around her face like our words were flies. Plus Asha's good friend Nandi lives here and was happy to put us up. In the end, even Asha was susceptible to the promise of a good time on her birthday. Which is today.

So I woke up in a Portland attic just now—July next to me, Terra and Asha on a mattress on the other side of the large room. Terra was just waking too and she saw me, gave a little wave. I waved back and tiptoed down to the bathroom, wincing as the wood stairs squeaked.

As I boiled water for tea, I explored Nandi's house. An orange lounge room with stereo and musical instruments. A book nook with shelves covering one whole wall. Comfy living room and couch. Books stacked everywhere. Canvases propped all around, in progress.

There's even a meditation closet. I had to laugh. *These queers and their closets.*

I grabbed my pot of tea and Sadie and went out back. Found a quilt on the soft grass and lay down on my back, looking up at the giant oak tree above me, its branches reaching protectively over the yard.

We missed the Fourth entirely, on the road, fine by me. I worried about Sharky, with the fireworks, texted Ingy to see if he was okay. She texted back that he seemed unconcerned. I hoped that Lily and Brix were having fun in Zion, seemed to remember they would be returning soon.

10:30 a.m.

Terra came out back a little while after I did, her short red hair sticking up like a toddler's, but her glasses, which I'd never seen her in, making her look older. She has a physical grace, a lovely way of carrying herself that I envy.

Confidence. Even in her T-shirt and sweats.

She settled down next to me and I shut my laptop. I offered her some tea, which she declined. She doesn't drink caffeine, which I don't understand.

I lay back again. "This grass is so comfortable."

She ran her fingers through it. "It's called creeping soft grass."

She looked up into the tree, like me, like it held some secrets, or some answers.

Then she left to go give Asha a happy birthday kiss.

July 6

8:47 a.m.

Nandi's backyard is my new favorite place. I'm back here again, the first one awake. We hung out here most of the day yesterday, celebrated Asha's 29 years on the planet with psychedelic mushrooms that Nandi grew from a kit. Not a lot, just a few small ones each.

Nandi's great. She's in her 40s, very funny and smart. She and Asha met when they were kids, in India, and they have a sweet comfort together, like sisters. Nandi's tall and busty, with glowing skin and big brown eyes, and these wild moods—like you never know what you're gonna get.

That intense energy can be intoxicating, but I could never be with someone like that. July's steady calm, I can trust it. She gets emotional, sure…but she's the same person today that she was yesterday, and she'll be the same person tomorrow.

Nandi's friends came over for a little barbecue, including a 4-year-old girl. We didn't know she was coming when we ate the shrooms, but we tried to stay somewhat normal for her sake. Nandi found a bunch of strings of lights in her basement, and together we all untangled and hung them. Then Nandi plugged them in, and the yard came alive, color snaking all around us. Asha laughed and smiled at me and I felt such a joy deep in my chest, like we were okay.

Even though it was her birthday, Asha insisted on making her mom's samosas with green apple chutney. Nandi made shish kabobs with teriyaki tempe, mushrooms, tomatoes, and she barbecued ears of corn in their husks.

Portland is, like, blessed. Even Asha is happy here. She's like a whole other person—she and Terra are of course talking about moving here. I know I couldn't handle the gray skies. Asha likes gray.

We had Voodoo Doughnuts for dessert, the Voodoo Doll with a candle glowing in its heart for Asha. We sang to her and she blew it out. Everyone took a doughnut, and we all shared.

Then we walked down the street to watch a Fifth of July fireworks show from a big church lawn at the end of Nandi's block. The fireworks went off down at the end of Hawthorne, like if you headed for downtown you'd drive right into them.

I held July's hand the whole way. She was my protection against the big, bad, sober world. We settled back on the lawn and shared a red plastic cup of champagne, watching the fireworks reflect off it.

As we walked back, Nandi's neighbors set off some more fireworks on the street. We watched them and then did some sparklers in front of Nandi's house, her gift for Asha.

Asha made circles above Terra's head, a halo. July conducted our choir. Nandi sat with her friend's kid, showing her how to draw a star. I turned around in circles with mine: trailing behind me, faster and faster, spinning myself away from them, running from the light.

I remembered the sparklers Yuki and Clara and I lit at the beach, our last night together. I made a big W with the last of the light, just like I had that night. The traces burned into my retinas.

I blinked and there it was again. W.

But when I blinked again it was gone.

Terra and I had another good talk tonight. It was 90 degrees out and we wanted to walk to the restaurant. Everyone else wanted to drive, so we decided to meet them there. We walked slowly, marveling over the trees and flowers. It's like a jungle up here.

I'm pretty sure Asha hasn't talked to Terra about what happened with Patrick, because Terra is completely open with me. It's almost like I can still be close with Asha, through Terra.

"So, we're talking about having a baby," Terra said, cutting to the chase. "I'm not exactly sure how that happened. Sometimes I feel like Asha's pulled one over on me."

I laughed. "She's a sneaky one. Do you want kids?"

"Yeah, I do. But she's ready, like, now. And I don't think I am yet."

"Have you told her that?"

"Kind of. But she's already talking details. There are ways to insert donated sperm at home, apparently."

"The turkey baster method?"

"There's apparently a long curved syringe, but yeah. I have a couple friends I could ask to donate."

"Wow, exciting." I figured I might as well be supportive, but there was a sickening envy spreading through me.

"Yeah. I know I want kids, and I think we'd be good parents. It's just, I'm only 23. I have so much I want to do still."

"Of course."

"But I don't know if she can wait. It's like now or never."

"But she must know you have to make this decision together." I was annoyed with Asha.

Terra was a little surprised. "She does. I just need to get more clear about what I want." She smiled. "Have you and July talked about kids?"

"Yeah...I don't want them." I didn't want to get into a discussion about it.

"Really? I thought you liked kids—weren't you a teacher in Japan?"

"I was. But I don't really like babies."

"How does July feel?"

"She accepts it," I snapped. Truth is, she only brought it up once. Early days in the attic, she asked if I want kids, and I said, "No. I don't." A normal person would have answered this question with more warmth, curiosity. A normal person would ask, Do *you* want kids? But I didn't want to know the answer, so I didn't ask.

We saw some planters with veggies growing in them on the sidewalk and sat down on one to have a smoke. She's been smoking Nat Shermans, they're delicious. The veggies were flourishing. It felt tropical, with the heat and all the vibrant plants.

I felt Terra watching me. I could tell she wanted to ask me something.

"What?" I asked, irritated.

"Did something happen to make you not like babies?" She looked so sad, like this was the worst thing she could imagine.

I didn't want to lie to her, especially since she asked with so much care. I've used up a whole life's worth of lies this year, and all it's done is keep me away from the people around me. That's not what I want anymore.

I stared out at the street, which was quiet and clean. I picked a cherry tomato and ate it. Terra was waiting patiently, trailing her hands over the leaves of some underground vegetable.

I wanted to tell her the truth. I wanted her to hug me and comfort me. I wanted her to understand me.

I took a drag. I said, "Something happened, yes. I can't tell you about it right now, but I will. Thank you for asking.

I actually really appreciate it."

It was true. It felt good to have her care about me enough to brave my cold front and just fucking ask. I handed her the cigarette.

We got up then and walked to the restaurant. After dinner they all went to check out some lesbian bar and July and I went off on our own. We took a walk and ended up at this fancy pastry place, sitting at a table on the sidewalk with a dessert out of a Tim Burton film.

I wanted to tell July everything then. I watched her across the table and considered it. But July is the place I go to feel good. If I share my demons with her, where will be my safe place be?

As I was deliberating what I would say, she grabbed my arm, scooped up a swirl of caramel mousse, and wrote i <3 u on my naked forearm. I went and sat in her lap and sucked the rest off her finger, then made her lick the mousse off my arm.

Then I dabbed some caramel on her nose. Which led to her smushing a big bite of cake in my mouth and me pushing her down to the ground, us licking caramel and chocolate off each other's faces, me straddling her on the sidewalk.

Customers in the shop staring out at us like we we're animals in a zoo. We're in Portland, and *we're* the freaks.

We walked back to Nandi's and went in through the back. They were still out drinking, so we had the house to ourselves. We decided to take a bath in Nandi's giant claw-foot, and had some really creative sex in there. Now why don't we do that at home?

July 7

10 a.m.

Woke up early again. As I stood in the kitchen waiting for the water to boil, looking out over the backyard, out of nowhere something broke in me. The dam I'd built inside me just collapsed, and when the emotion came I couldn't stop it. I couldn't breathe. Like something wanted out.

I was pacing Nandi's kitchen, shaking and sobbing. Afraid of someone waking up, witnessing my mess.

I remembered the meditation closet. I turned off the kettle and went in, shut the door behind me, and sat down on the pillow, in complete darkness. I had to be quiet, since Nandi's room is right next door, but I was hyperventilating, so I pulled off my sweatshirt and breathed into it like a paper bag, drool and snot going everywhere but my crazy-sounding crying muffled at least.

I held the sweatshirt to me like a baby. I cradled it and cried.

If she had lived, she would have been about that size by now. The size of my bunched-up hoodie.

There in the closet, it felt like she was lodged in my heart. Like she'd traveled up instead of out, to live in my heart instead of my womb. And I knew that she would be there forever.

I leaned back against the wall behind me, tried to breathe. No one came for me. I told myself I would get up when I heard the attic floor creak above me. But it never did, so I stayed.

I saw horrible things in there.

I saw pieces of Willow on a silver tray in the hospital. A little arm the size of an edamame pod.

I saw Sean walking in to my note saying I'd left, and

sitting there immobilized.

I saw my students' faces when Haruka told them I'd left, tough little Hana crying.

I saw everything I missed by running away, a parade of memories I never got to have. If I had just been there to have them, instead of running, maybe it would have been easier. Things could have happened like they're supposed to: denial, acceptance, grief, etc. Instead I ran, trying to postpone the process.

The gods of Nandi's altar told me this. I couldn't see them, but I felt around for them, for something to hold onto. Finally my hand settled on a statue, and I picked it up and felt it. When I came to the trunk I knew it was Ganesha. Remover of obstacles.

I held him so tight. I pushed his trunk into my heart, where the pain was. He was about the size Willow was when she died. I held onto Ganesha for dear life, pushed him between my breasts, and apologized, begged, prayed to him in my head.

I prayed to be okay again, for it all to be okay. For a long time I just pleaded with Ganesha, "Please, please, please, please, please…"

And then after what felt like hours, the nag champa having suffused my system, I opened the door and let in a sliver of light, just enough to see. I put Ganesha back and thanked him, piled the pink flower petals back up around his feet and took one, put it in my pocket. Then I closed the door and came out and made my tea, grabbed Sadie, and came back out to the backyard.

Feeling very calm now. Cleared out.

My last morning writing in Nandi's backyard. We're driving home today. I don't want to leave.

July 8

I drove most of the way back to Oakland last night, July in the passenger seat playing DJ, flipping through her binders of CDs for just the right thing. Despite her occasional disdain, I knew she didn't want to totally alienate Asha and Terra, and that she wanted to please me.

It was a good thing for everyone that we were back on our own in the biodieselmobile, safe to indulge in our crazy love. We're the only ones who understand. J and I held hands most of the way home.

And now T'n'A seemed to be on to logistics. I heard Asha tell Terra how big women's breasts get in the weeks before the birth, and how then they grow even more in the weeks after the baby is born, and in the rearview mirror I saw Terra frown. She's proud of her flat-fronted body, and Asha loves it too. Asha's boobs getting big, though—that's something they can both agree on.

As we drove over the pass and into Cali, July put on Sinéad O'Connor, turned it up loud, and rolled her window down.

> *There's life outside your mother's garden*
> *There's life beyond your wildest dreams*

She watched the hills of Oregon turn into the hills of California, and I thought she looked pleased to be so far from home. The music filled the car to capacity and then floated out into the world.

> *Pick up those dancing shoes*
> *Kick off those wedding blues*
> *These are the ways you can choose*

She looked over at me, and the wind whipped my ponytail, and in that moment I felt that I was just how she saw me.

The wind picked up the pink flower petal, which I had put on the dash as we left Portland, and it sailed out her window with the music.

My last check from Hikari International Preschool was waiting in the mail when we got back. It was much more than I was expecting, $3,670. It included the security deposit on the apartment, I realized.

Just in time, because my bank account was getting dangerously dry after Portland and I still have no idea what to do for work.

I now have $5,074 until I find a job.

July 9

J and I had sex in her barber chair today.

I was missing her, so I rode my bike over to visit her at work. She was just finishing up with her last client, a beefy gay tattoo artist that she had a sweet rapport with.

When he left she locked the front door so no one else would come in. I climbed into her chair and asked her to cut my bangs. I watched her in the mirror as she tucked a smock around me and expertly cut them to mid-forehead. She was showing off a little. So sexy.

Then she pulled the smock away and started sweeping up the day's hair. I brushed myself off and went over to the front of the shop, kneeled in one of the chairs by the window, and gazed out at the other shops in the alley.

I felt like I was in the 1950s. The bebop on the stereo, the cursive Alley Cuts sign on the window, my high ponytail and poufy poodle-type skirt, my hot girlfriend in her slicked-back pompadour, tight black T-shirt and Levi's....

I lowered the blinds on one window, and then the next. I looked over to where July was finishing her sweeping, eyeing me. I stepped out of my shoes and walked slowly toward her, reaching under my skirt as I did, pulling my underwear off and flinging them toward her. They landed on the counter, polka dots atop scissors and clippers.

I pulled July to me by her belt loop, kissed her hard, then pushed her back into her chair and climbed on top. She lifted the back of my skirt, checked out my ass in her mirror behind me, next to a photo she'd taped there of me in a bikini and sunglasses.

She put her hand inside me then. We didn't need any lube. I touched myself, and she watched me in the mirror, moving up and down on her hand. She pulled up my turquoise tank top and took my breast in her mouth, and it felt so good I couldn't stop her. If any milk came out, she didn't say anything.

Soon I was coming. I held onto the back of the chair, the side of my head pressed against hers, and I bucked against her hand again and again, crying into her ear, "You're so good, baby. You're so good." Then I dropped my body down into her lap, and reached down into her pants. She was as wet as I was. I kissed her neck and ears and whispered what I knew she wanted to hear. She watched us in the mirror, and soon she was coming too.

I sat back, took her face in my hands, and kissed her. I held her precious face and looked into her endless amber eyes and told her I loved her.

Then she locked up and we went for organic ice cream. Burnt Caramel for me, Sweet Cream for her.

July 10

Brix is dead. I just woke up in Lily's bed. She's still asleep, so I came up to write this down. It's like a bad dream. Oh god, I wish it was just a dream.

July and I went to the White Horse last night, for a burlesque show that Lexy's girlfriend was in. Even as tasseled boobs twirled in front of my eyes like those hypnosis circles, I couldn't get into it, so we left early and decided to sleep at July's, since Lexy was staying with her girlfriend after the show. I went home to grab some clothes and a movie, and walked in to Asha sobbing on the couch, Terra looking terrified.

"Brix is dead," Terra said quietly. "Lily's in her room."

I sat down on the chair beneath me, all my strength dropping away. Terra told me Merry had brought Lily home a couple hours earlier, had called up the stairs for help. Asha and Terra rushed over to find Lily standing with crutches at the bottom of the stairs.

"Lily didn't say a word," Terra said. "We took her straight to her room, got her into bed. Merry asked her if she wanted to be alone, to try and get some sleep, and Lily nodded. So we left her in there." At this Asha started crying harder.

I nodded at Terra, left them, and knocked on Lily's door, walked in without waiting for a response. She was lying on her back, staring at the ceiling, and when I walked in she started to cry and held her arms out to me like a baby. I sat down and hugged her, and when I pulled away I saw her paled face, her bruised-looking under-eyes. She looked like she'd been up for weeks, and her hair was dirty and matted. I smoothed it out and held her to me as she cried and cried, and finally fell asleep.

I texted July that I wasn't coming over, carefully so as not to disturb Lily, my arm still underneath her. If you can sit through the discomfort of your limbs falling asleep, eventually they just become numb.

Lily woke in the middle of the night. I did too, confused to find myself in her bed. Then I remembered. I sat up, switched on her globe lamp. The oceans of the world glowed a gentle blue.

She seemed calmer, pushed herself up slowly, wincing. I put a pillow behind her back, so she was propped against the wall like a broken doll, legs sticking out in front of her, the right one in a cast. Then she started to speak, scared but steady.

"We were having a really good trip. Brix planned it perfectly. We were riding like 30 miles a day, stopping at streams and rivers to cool off and wash. We got really dirty with all that dust."

So it was dust matting her hair. She had let me smooth out the tangles before she fell asleep, but she hadn't said a word until now. The muting of Lily's expressive voice had been as alarming as the lack of life in her face. I was happy to hear her speak, but her voice had lost all its life too. The story carried her, created an urgency.

"We swam in these beautiful streams and waterfalls…in the Narrows, this incredible gorge. Water gushes through, these crazy purple flowers called shooting stars covering the walls. All these families with kids on summer vacation—and we're in there washing our clothes.

"Then we'd get back on the road and the dust would swirl around us and we'd be dirty again. But we saw so many amazing things, Nara, so many beautiful places, and so many animals. Turkeys and foxes and deer. One night we saw a mountain lion.

"We slept in the back country, as far away from people as we could get, and without the tent fly, so we could see the sky. So many shooting stars. And there were these crazy hoodoos, these big rock formations that look like aliens. It was like being on the moon."

She was looking down at her hands, holding them out like she didn't recognize them.

"It was like coming home, to a home I never knew I had. He would show me these awesome places, and they felt familiar, just from hearing him talk about them. He camped at Zion all the time in high school, and he talked about it a lot. We'd been planning this trip ever since we met."

She grimaced and pulled at her cast leg, tucked her left leg under her to turn toward me.

I reached over and took her hand, held it between mine. "You don't have to tell me what happened."

"I do." She pulled her hand away, tucked it under her. I tried not to be hurt. She wanted someone to take record of the story, but she needed to be alone in it, to get herself back there.

She breathed in deep, and leaned her head against the wall, exhaling slowly. Closed her eyes. "One day we were tired so we just lay around all day, reading and singing. Beatles, mostly."

I remembered her "Jealous Guy" cover at that first show at the Nomad, her and Brix whistling the bridge together.

"We were dreading going home. We had only two days left.

"That evening, Brix got antsy. He said he wanted to take a walk to some rocks, not too far from our camp. I was sleepy from the heat, so I kissed him and went into the tent for a nap. Before I zipped it up, I looked out at him walking away and I wanted to go with him. But I was feeling lazy, so I just watched him go."

She froze. And then, again, I watched her breathe, bring herself back. I said, "It'll be okay," and she nodded. It had to be, because Lily was not letting herself break down. She swatted the sheets away from her.

"I read for a while, and then I fell asleep. When I woke up, it was dark. I went outside, and there was no Brix, no fire, no nothing but me and the stars. So many stars.

"I called for him. My voice was so loud in all that quiet. There was no response. Nothing.

"It had gotten cold and he'd left with just a T-shirt on. I put my sweatshirt on and grabbed his."

She shivered, her body quivering, and I tucked her blankets around her. I handed her the glass of water from the table by the bed, then picked up a pill bottle sitting there—Xanax. I rattled it questioningly and she shook her head no. I resisted the urge to ask if I could have one.

She closed her eyes, and described what she was seeing. "It was an almost full moon. Our bikes were still there. But no Brix."

Her voice broke when she said his name, then she set her jaw and continued. "I put his sweatshirt around my waist and grabbed the flashlight from his pack. I didn't think to bring anything else. I was still disoriented from my nap, and the dark, and the cold, and him being gone… the world was so different from how I'd left it. I wasn't even sure which direction to go, I hadn't really paid attention to where he said he was going. I remembered him mentioning rocks, but there were lots of rocks, everywhere I looked there were big piles of rocks.

"I called his name again. My voice sounded so horrible, I hated the sound of it, the panic. I didn't want him to hear it and know how worried I was…and I knew if he was nearby he would have heard me and called back, if he could have."

She was totally tranced out, her eyes looking at me and seeing desert. At least when she was talking part of her was in the room with me.

"Go on," I said, and her pupils came back into focus.

"I shone the flashlight out into the desert, picked the biggest pile of rocks and started walking toward them. It was scary out there, in the dark. Completely silent, except for the sand crunching under my feet, bats whizzing by now and then. I started to run after a while, and when I got to the rocks I was out of breath. I looked back and could just barely see our tent in the moonlight.

"I called to him again, and this time I heard his voice, very faintly—I couldn't tell what he said, but I knew it was him. I called again, louder this time, and I heard him again. It sounded like the grunt we teach women in labor to make through their contractions. I kept calling to him, and he kept responding—once he said 'Lily!' I climbed toward the sound of him, which sounded like it was coming from underneath the rocks.

"Climbing them in the dark was difficult, I kept slipping. I was moving too fast and I twisted my foot."

She threw a dirty look at her cast.

"So stupid. It hurt, and of course I shouldn't have been walking on it, but there was no way I was gonna stop. So I just kept moving toward Brix's voice.

"He was under a big pile, on his side, his torso pinned between two rocks. I scrambled down there, so happy to see him. When I got to him I crouched down and held his head in my hands and kissed him. When I pulled my hand away there was blood on my hand. A lot of blood. I wiped it on a rock, didn't mention it to Brix. Just smiled at him, at his beautiful face, which I could hardly see. The moon didn't shine down there.

"He was delirious to see me, laughing and not making sense. He said—what was it? 'I thought I'd lost myself too much for you to find me.' He had been trying to keep himself awake, to call to me in case I came.

"He said he couldn't feel his arm, the one pinned underneath him. That scared me, but it was also good, because when I pried him out it didn't hurt. I knew I should be careful of his spine—all my emergency training rushed through my head. But what were my options? He's stuck under an enormous pile of rocks, no one around for miles, it's late, and my foot is messed up. It was starting to really hurt.

"I tried to wedge my arm under his torso. It took a couple tries, but finally I figured out the right angle and got him out of there. He sat back against a rock, one side of his hair all goofy from the blood, dirt all over his glasses. He gave me a big, happy smile and said, 'I'm free!' I was panting, and laughing, and finally able to hug him. We laughed and held each other, happy to be together again. I thought everything would be okay."

She was propelled by the momentum of the story, telling it quickly now.

"I put his sweatshirt on him, leaving the arm he couldn't move hanging. I put his hood on. His skin was ice-cold. He'd been protected from the wind down there, but with the blood loss…. I tried not to think about it, tried to focus on what to do next.

"I had to get him back to the tent. There at least I had a phone. We had no service, but maybe I could ride somewhere, try to get help…. I told Brix this, and he nodded. I didn't tell him about my foot. I just told him to follow me.

"I pointed the flashlight for myself, and then back for

him, with every rock we climbed. It was *such* a slow process. I was favoring my left leg, but at least I had both arms to work with…he just had the one, so it was really awkward. I knew I should wrap his arm up, but I couldn't take the time, plus I didn't have anything to wrap it with.

"He told me he had a map in his pocket. 'The Wonderland of Rocks,' he told me. 'That's what this place is called.'

"I laughed at how prepared he was, and how useless a map was to us at that point. I told him, 'It's a wonderland, all right. And you fell down the rabbit hole.'

"He said, 'Curiouser and curiouser.'"

She smiled, remembering.

"We finally made it down—it probably took us an hour. Brix lay down on his back in the sand. He moved his legs and his one good arm up and down. 'Sand angel,' he said. I lay down next to him and did the same with my arms and one good leg—a couple of crippled sand angels.

"We lay there looking up—it seemed like there were more stars than sky—getting our strength back. We saw three shooting stars, we made three wishes. My wishes were all for the same thing: *Let Brix make it back okay.* I guess I should have been more specific.

"We did finally make it back okay, to our camp—it took a long time, but it was easy compared to the rocks. We were hungry, so when we got back I made a small fire and heated some chili, and we had the last granola bars for dessert. He drank a lot of water, and I tried not to worry about our supply. I used almost the last of it to clean his head. The blood had dried, but there was a lot of it. I wrapped it in a clean long-sleeve thermal top.

"And then I had no more energy for anything else. My foot was really hurting but I was just praying that it would be better in the morning. It had to be, or I wouldn't be able to bike for help, or ride to a place with cell service. The last time we'd had service had been two days earlier. We hadn't seen anyone in almost that long.

"The only thing I could do was warm us up. We were so tired. His eyes kept falling closed. I got us into our sleeping bags and looked at each other and said 'I love you' at the same time like we'd been practicing. Then he closed his eyes and fell asleep, and I watched him breathe for a while.

"That thing about not letting people who have a concussion fall asleep is a myth, but I still didn't feel good about leaving him. Finally I couldn't stay awake anymore, and I fell asleep too.

"In the morning he was gone. It was TBI, they said, traumatic brain injury. I had even tested his level of consciousness, on our walk back from the rocks, and he did okay.

There was nothing more I could have done. There was no one to help us. I just wanted us to be together—that was the important thing. To be together, and warm… I know he didn't suffer, because he would have woken me. He just fell asleep, and never woke up."

"Oh, Lil," I said, willing my tears back, my heart about to explode. She was looking down at the quilt, her face hard and unmoving. "Let's lie down," I said, gently pulling her to her back. I asked if she needed anything, and she asked me to stay with her. I smoothed her hair away from her face until she fell into sleep—twitching violently, then settling.

As I switched off the globe lamp, I remembered the day I'd walked in and seen Lily and Brix sleeping where she and I were now. Maybe they'd been dreaming together of their hoodoo home. I imagined them there and drifted off, dreaming of their dreams.

July 12

Lily is obsessing about what happened in the desert, going over and over it in her mind. Like she needs to relive it to remind herself that there was no other way.

I'm even doing it. I read the story she told me, where I recorded it here, and think of other ways it could have gone. Lily screams, at the campfire, after getting Brix back—she screams into the quiet dark, as loud as she can, "Help!" and some lonely traveler comes to their aid. Alternate endings fill my head, enticing me with the illusion of control.

But there weren't any alternatives, or Lily, who loved Brix more than anything, would have found them. In the end I have to believe in the story, in the way it went down being the only way it could.

Her foot was broken, and of course she'd made it worse by walking on it, back to the tent with him and then the next day to get help with his body. And with no water, in hundred-degree heat, so that by the time she finally flagged someone down she had heatstroke too.

At the hospital, after she stabilized and her foot was set, she arranged for Brix's body to be taken to his family and called Merry to help her drive the wagon and bikes back. Once she was back here, home, she didn't leave her bed for days, except to use the bathroom.

I've been helping her get in and out of the bath, and washing her hair. We put jojoba oil in her hair and on her skin. I try not to look at her body, at how skinny she's gotten, at how beautiful she is regardless. I try to be all business, to think about what Lily needs and not be weird. She told me she's lucky to have roommates, and it's true, it makes it easier for us to help her. But I know her friends would have come from great distances to help.

Most of them found out about Brix via Facebook. Lily made a memorial page for him. Virtual grieving. His friends from all over the country, together in one place, even it's just the Internet. I think it's good for her, to put faces to names she's only heard, to receive the support of so many people who loved him. To feel less alone in the utter confusion of his absence.

He was just here. And now he's gone.

July 17

It's been a week since Lily got home. There were moments in the first few days when I thought she might not get through this. That she might not try. It's understandable—the stress her mind, heart, body are under are really too much for anyone to withstand, even a person like Lily who's designed for crisis.

But now she has a new look: focused on my face, looking into it as if for clues. Or not seeing me at all, seeing desert, getting lost. I have to pull her back, say her name, snap my fingers.

Asha has been too caught up in her own emotions to be much help. July has also been extremely unhelpful. She's probably jealous of Lily, of the time I'm spending with her. She knows I have strong feelings for her. But whatever, I told her I'm needed here and she'll have to be patient. I can only think about Lily and Brix right now.

Lily is also having some weird allergic reaction, she says to grief. Like it's infesting her skin, and when she scratches it, big welts appear. They look like something inside her is fighting to get out. She wrote BRIX all over her body today, with her fingernails, on her forearms and thighs and chest. I didn't see her do it but I saw the welts, his name in raised letters and her fingers running over them.

She told me that sometimes, stoned, she'd had the feeling that everything was wrong in the world. She'd always called it paranoia. Now she knows it was depression. Intellectually she knows there are good, positive things and people, but emotionally they hold no resonance, no meaning. They confuse her, actually. It isn't right that the world should keep moving, rotating. It seems insensitive of all those strangers to be going to work, picking up their kids from school, watching the World Cup.

If it wasn't for us, the disconnect between Lily and the rest of the world would be even more complete. We're a middle zone—somewhat more functional than she is, but still in shock.

She told me that more than one of her friends, upon hearing the news, thought, *Anyone but Brix.* But she witnessed his end so completely and totally, there'll be no magical thinking for her. He's gone, and she was unable to stop it happening. And so her pain is threefold—the heartbreak of his absence, her guilt that she didn't do enough, and the physical pain she's in from her efforts to save him. She knows she pushed her body as far as was humanly possible. She knows that no one of Brix's friends could have saved him. She was the only one, and she hadn't been able to… which has to mean it was his time to go.

It was no one's fault. She has to keep reminding herself of this. He's gone, but there's no one to blame. Her loving face had been the last thing he'd seen. He hadn't been murdered, or killed in a car crash, hunks of metal piercing his beautiful body. That consoles her. These thoughts, she told me, are as close as she can get to thinking positively. They're better than the desperation that pulls at her. She knows she could easily go under if she doesn't actively fight it…and her inability to move around means she has to use her mind to fight now.

I took another one of Lily's Xanax tonight. I've taken a few—they help me stay calm for her. I put one of her Oxycontin in my pocket and brought it up here too. Just in case.

July 23

Today was Lily's birthday. She didn't mention it, but I had written it down on the calendar in the kitchen. She didn't want to do anything, but I insisted on making her dinner. Potato pancakes. Asha made applesauce, and Terra shared her new home brew. July came too but didn't stay long after dinner. She seems nervous around Lily, and I was relieved when she left.

Not that it was a big hootenanny. We lit candles and listened to records, smoked cigarettes on the back porch. We all knew pot would be too much. Asha set up her massage table in the living room and gave Lily a massage, and Terra and I played cards. When we saw tears falling from the face cradle to the wood floors below, we just looked at each other. There was no point trying to stop them. She's going to have to cry them all.

After the massage, Claudia and Ingy brought up a cake that Claudia made. Chocolate cake with lemon frosting, which was somehow perfect. On top was a little frog eraser that Ingy found at the Japanese store.

We sang, and ate cake, and drew flowers on Lily's cast. She sat in her robe on the couch, talking to Claudia while she drank one of Terra's beers and the rest of us played gin rummy. I taught Ingy how and her first hand she got gin. She threw up her hands and stood up to do a little dance, singing, "That's right, suckas."

Then Ingy remembered where she was. She put her hands in her lap as if by force and sat back down, her face quickly stripped of its smile, her eyes wide and sad as they looked over at Lily.

Lily was oblivious, her eyes lost in the candle flame on the coffee table. I imagined she was seeing that final campfire. No one else knows the story of that night. I figure she'll tell them when she's ready. The knowing is more of a curse than a blessing.

July 26

I asked Lily if I could take her to the Black beauty parlor as a birthday gift. To get anything she wanted.

She wanted a perm. She hadn't had one since she was in high school, wanted to cut off all the old stuff and make the rest curly.

So today we went to a salon in Temescal, run by this super sweet older Black guy and his younger sister. We were the only ones there and they laughed enthusiastically at all of Lily's jokes. I was surprised she could still make them. It was her first time in public after getting back from the desert, and I think she didn't know how to be anything other than her old charming self.

I sat in the back, at one of the dryer chairs, and watched her up on her throne, commanding all three mirrors with a straight spine. Like she was fighting the depression, pushing it back, away from her. Her cast with our flowers on it and her other foot in her Converse with rainbow laces were propped on the chair's foot rest.

When they were taking out the curlers, she told them, "I lost my boyfriend."

Immediately they both stopped and waited for her to say more. "What happened, honey?" the woman said.

Lily said, "I just wanted you guys to know. I mean, I don't want to pretend like it didn't happen."

The man said, "Thanks for telling us, love. You need anything you let us know. Want some water?"

Lily said yes.

The woman said, "You want some scotch?" We all laughed, and Lily nodded. "Sorry, girl, but we ain't got no scotch."

Lily smiled. But then she looked over at me, and the

smile fell away.

It took forever, the perm, hours and hours. It seemed to me that they kept doing the same thing over and over again: dry and then add product, dry and then add product, again and again. Lily was so patient though, she just sat and watched them in the mirror, looked around, her eyes taking in the many bottles of product lining the ceiling and stashed all over, the blue and pink and green curlers popping out of plastic drawers like preschool toys. I imagined that the world had returned to color for her, the woman's candy-pink shirt and the red chairs and the bright blue walls. Then sometimes she'd close her eyes for a while, go back inside. Guessing it's black-and-white in there.

I read all the magazines in the shop, including the hair magazines. I admired the hair extensions hanging in plastic bags on the wall, hair from all over the world, and a case of eyelashes on the counter.

I walked to get us all organic ice cream, at the corner by July's barbershop. I remembered the sex in her chair, and eating ice cream with her afterward, and riding bikes home together after that, sore on my bike seat.

We've only had sex once since Lily got back, and I was so distracted by the thought of Lily in her room below us, I didn't come. I didn't want to.

I thought about going in and saying hi to July, but I had to get the ice cream back to Lily and the salon siblings, and I wasn't up to seeing the pain in her eyes.

Lily's hair is super cute, short with a collection of tiny curls, like a succulent, springing out into the world.

August 2

In my bathroom just now, I heard Lily talking to Brix. Her bedroom window must be open, and my bathroom window was open, so I could hear her pretty clearly. I just sat there, feeling like I should stop listening, give her privacy, but instead I got really quiet, straining to hear.

She said, "I miss you so much." That's how I knew she was talking to him.

She said, "I'm sorry."

I wanted to go down and comfort her, but I was afraid then she'd know I heard her. So I just sat on the toilet, unable to move.

She said, "I can feel you."

Where did he go? How can it be that he's not coming back? How are we supposed to accept this?

There's no one to explain it to us.

August 8

Chatted with Sean on Facebook for a couple minutes tonight. I friended him with my new name.

I didn't tell him about Brix. He and I have enough shit to deal with. I feel like in our chat we started to, though, a little. Maybe it was easier, chatting online, not having to see each other or hear each other's voice. It seemed like he said goodbye kind of abruptly—maybe he was mad. But I think it's okay. I think it's better than nothing, better than pretending we're all good.

He said he didn't think we would have worked out, and he wouldn't have wanted to be a single parent, so it's better this way. I must admit, as much as I agree, it was still hard to hear.

August 8

I've been caring for Lily. Cooking and cleaning. Going out only when we need something, so I'm here in case she needs me. It's hard for her to get around, and she's still having a lot of pain and refusing pain meds. Refusing any meds. I've been taking one here and there. I haven't asked, it feels weird to, but I'm sure she would say yes.

The Xanax helps me not to worry, to stay here where I'm needed, to stay present. On the Oxycontin, I feel so peaceful, like we're in a houseboat.

An emergency has such a precious quality, of time having stopped. The clarity of knowing what you are doing with every second of your day. Like this house is sacred, and no one else in the world can understand.

I've been sleeping with her most nights. She's having trouble getting to sleep and staying asleep. I give her the same herbs she gave me when I first got here. And when she wakes up at 3:30 like I used to, I sing her back to sleep or tell her a story.

She's decided to take her fall semester off. I helped her drop her classes. I told her I'll put my first semester off till the spring too. She didn't fight me on it.

There's a lot of business around Brix's death to be dealt with. His mom and sister are staying in the cob house, going through his things. They want to split up his stuff in a way that's fair to Lily.

So we've been driving back and forth, from our house to East Oakland, bringing many boxes of Brix back to our place. Lily is indiscriminate, wants anything and everything of his that no one else cares about, while anything they want she gives up readily. Her room, and our living room, are becoming overrun with boxes, and tools, and bike parts, and other greasy things that Asha and I are secretly alarmed by. Our sweet little house is turning into a garage. Of course we don't dare tell Lily it bothers us.

I read Joan Didion's *The Year of Magical Thinking*. In it she says that the only book that helped her when her husband died was Emily Post's 1922 book of etiquette, because it includes practical suggestions such as to bring grieving people some soup, and just hand it to them, because if you ask them they will say they don't want it.

So I make Lily veggie soup, without asking her if she wants it. I play her favorite music, music with gentle life in it. I make her world look nice, keep it clean, bring flowers, open her windows, let the air in. I don't ask her to make decisions.

I want to try and save her, the way she saved me. When I got here, she showed me a way away from the edge. Now I have the chance to do the same for her—of course I have to try.

I'm enjoying having Lily to myself, I'll admit it. This was what I wanted, when I arrived: more Lily, always more Lily. But I want to make it clear, to myself, to whoever's listening—this isn't what I wanted! Those times I wondered, *What if it weren't for Brix?* This is not what I wanted.

I haven't talked to Asha in days. When she's here she and Terra mostly stay in their room. It's like Brix's death has disabled something in her. Lily, who knows her better than me or Terra, seems as perplexed by it as we are. I don't really mind, because things have been weird between me and Asha for a while, and I haven't told anyone my secrets yet, like I told her I would.

And July…I don't really want her to come over. I can't deal with a big talk. So I'm asking her to wait, staying in touch via text, telling her I'll be back soon.

My shit will just have to wait. It'll be there when I'm ready for it.

August 18

July and I had sex today. I brought her some oatmeal chocolate chip cookies I'd made, her fave. Lexy was out, thank god. We went in July's room and were sitting on her bed and then all of a sudden we were devouring each other. It had been way too long.

I sobbed as I came. I didn't want to talk about it afterward, though. I just wanted to lie with her and look up into the ocean on her ceiling, imagine we were Freeda and Sherman, mermaid and merman, and we could swim far away from our houses and the death in them, together through the mysteries of the ocean, making love as we went.

And then we did, we did it again, slowly this time, and I shoved away the images of Lily in the bath, focused on July's ceiling and imagined us there, wrapped together and breathing through our gills and slipping through the water together, surrounded by all the creatures of the sea.

We came together for the first time, and the sounds we made were strangled, muted, like they were coming from underwater, or some other faraway place.

August 22

Brix would have loved his memorial. His big house and lovely yard so full of his friends and family, it overflowed onto the sidewalk. The beautiful book Lily made for all of us to record our thoughts and memories of him sat on a table just inside the door to the cob house. The house he just built.

I sat on the steps to his bed loft and waited for a chance to write in his book. The room was completely still, despite all the people passing through it. The only words were whispers. I'd close my eyes, holding onto the stairs he'd made, trying to absorb the last of his energy, and when I opened my eyes someone new would be with the book, I'd have missed my chance. So I let the idea go and just sat, reciting my poem for him in my head instead, then writing it on a gum wrapper I had in my pocket, like a fortune. I sat for hours, smelling the cool mud of the walls, holding the wood stairs, remembering him building it. I never even got to see him inside it.

Brix's favorite songs rang out through the back door of the main house, from his iPod through the house speakers. Finally Lily's frog song, which they'd recorded in the garage, came on and broke my spell, gave me the energy to get up, to leave Brix behind. I left the cob house and went up the back stairs and into the main house, looking for Lily.

On a side table in the kitchen, available to take, sat patches with Brix's face screened on them and stacks of photos of him, along with booklets of photos Lily had made from their trip to the desert. I picked out a few of each and put them in my pocket. There was food too, of course, and wine, and whiskey.

I saw a woman who must have been Brix's mom,

straightening the food and looking totally lost. I remembered him telling me that she'd been trying his whole life to make up for his dad's abuse. My heart was hurting, and I thought, *Imagine her heart.*

But I couldn't bring myself to talk to her. I could never find the right words, I would only make it worse.

July texted me that she was there, and I wove my way through the hippunks on the front steps to meet her out front. I hugged her and whispered hello.

I took her hand and we stopped to look at the big altar at the base of the wide steps up to the Craftsman. We'd draped the garage door with the yards of soft plaid flannel Lily had bought to make Brix a shirt, and left sewing pins for people to pin photos and recollections. Now the flannel was covered with his beautiful face, his beautiful life.

He was so alive. He had lived fully, his too-few years. My throat was hurting from fighting back the pain of knowing, finally, that he wasn't coming back.

At our feet were candles of every color, and sage and incense burning, watched over by a vanguard of hippunks in folding chairs on the sidewalk. And people had left offerings. Homemade seed packets, a little wolf figurine, several feathers, because Brix had loved birds, a perfect sand dollar, chapbooks, stones, coins…somebody had left an AA chip. Lots and lots of flowers, on the altar and all around on the sidewalk, in vases and jars and mugs.

I led July up the front steps, and there was Lily on the couch on the porch, surrounded like a guru by her devotees. I hadn't seen her since I'd helped her put the altar together several hours earlier. I hugged her, and she started breaking all over me, shaking, sobbing. I was aware of July standing behind me, and pulled away before Lily was ready for me to.

July hugged her then too, and as Lily looked over her shoulder at me, I was afraid she would never go back to being the old Lily, Lily full of light. That Lily is hard to remember.

Then July pulled away, and one of Lily's friends asked her something, and we left her to them, made our way through the big house and out back, where we found Asha and Terra sitting on hay bales in the yard, by the chickens in their cob hutch.

I looked over at Asha, her head on Terra's shoulder, tears silently drenching Terra's shirt. She didn't look at me. We still haven't really spoken since Portland.

I sat with July on the next hay bale, dread settling into my belly. Such a familiar feeling.

Sitting in his backyard, the sun inexplicably shining, the four of us gazed at the chickens, not saying much. Communal grief. We were lucky, we had partners to get through this with. Lily is now missing the best person who could have helped her deal with his loss. It is this thought—that she had found someone who completed her, and now he's gone—that I keep getting stuck on.

The chickens squawking drowned out the pain of the people around me. I pulled the book of photos from my pocket and looked through them. Beautiful Brix, on his bike, making a fire, waving from a river. His last days, in Zion.

July told me that she and Asha were going inside to get something to eat, did I want anything? I shook my head and watched them go up the back steps and into the house. I was glad to be alone with Terra, and asked her how she'd been.

"It's been a crazy few weeks, Nara. I'm glad we can talk, because I have been totally freaking out. I didn't want to bother you. You're taking such good care of Lily." She gave me a grateful smile. "But basically, Asha has totally fallen apart. I don't think she knew how much she cared about Brix, since she's so anti-guy. It's like he was the last good one."

I thought, *Sean's a good one, too. Good just wasn't enough for me.*

Terra kept talking, about her dad's funeral, but I didn't hear her. I was thinking about how I never had a memorial for Willow. The closest I got was that night with Clara and Yuki, high on Vicodin and sake, swimming in the ocean in my undies. I thought about how Sean and I could have done something to honor her if I'd stayed and I felt a heavy blackness fill my head.

Maybe we still could.

No. It's too late.

When I returned, Terra was saying, "My heart was broken, but at least I finally was free of that place."

"This must be so different from your dad's memorial," I said, needing to change the subject.

"Oh, totally. It's much more relaxed." Terra smiled, looking around at the hippunks in the yard. The sun made it look like they were celebrating.

But it only made the darkness in me feel worse. A disease not even the sun could cure.

There we were with the chickens he raised, the house he built, the garden he planted.... What man could the world possibly replace him with? My heart swelled big and hard, and again I swallowed it back. I put my hand on Terra's shoulder for a second then pushed myself up.

I walked up to the chicken hutch and hung on it, watching the three hens waddle and cluck, oblivious. One was brownish-red, one was black, and one was a lighter brown with some white feathers around her bum. They were much bigger than the last time I'd seen them, when I was there helping with the cob house. I remembered Merry singing "Brix's Chickens" that day, Brix and Lily muddy and happy.

I looked up then and saw July watching me through the second-floor window of the house. "Come back," I mouthed and motioned her outside. Even from a distance, I saw her soften with hope.

She came down the back steps and I met her and took her hand, led her back to our place in the sun, me sitting next to Terra on the hay bale as July settled on the ground, between my legs. "Asha's in there talking to Brix's mom," July said, as she started to massage my feet.

I burst out laughing at the thought of Asha in there expertly doing the thing I couldn't even bring myself to attempt. Terra and July looked at me weird, but the laughing felt good, it broke my dark spell.

We were quiet for a while. I closed my eyes and enjoyed the feel of July's hands on me, the sun on my face.

"Sometimes I just can't believe this place I'm in," July said. "You can be anything you want here. It would have changed everything if I'd had that, growing up. Or at least in my 20s. Or 30s."

She fits right in, visually, with the rest of the pierced and the painted. She knows from talking to Brix that he had thought she was cool, had been interested in her and in her life. So I couldn't understand why she seemed so caught up with envying them.

And then she said what we were all thinking: "That good man is gone…." And a huge sob came out of her.

I scooted down to the ground and held her shaking body. Terra handed her the box of tissue I'd set on the hay bale, and all around the house, when I'd arrived earlier.

We were quiet for a while, July crying silently. I've only ever seen her cry like that when she told me about her brother. I wondered what Jamie's funeral was like.

I said, "I loved how Brix told jokes. He would say it, some goofy pun or whatever, and then he would wait quietly for you to get it. Like he could see the path the joke was taking to your brain and he could wait."

July pulled away and looked into my face, and with as much compassion as I could muster I said, "It's gonna be okay."

"Okay?" I asked her, and she nodded.

Terra reached over and squeezed July's shoulder, and I seized my opportunity and left them. I went inside to use the bathroom, and came back out with a couple vintage teacups of whiskey.

I saw Lily sitting with Merry on a blanket in the grass, their arms around each other like they were holding each other up. Someone had made Lily a daisy crown, and it sat atop her new curls.

I was feeling so much love for her.

I walked over and handed a teacup to each of them and sat down. They were both looking tired. Lily's boot cast had grass stains on it, among the flowers we'd drawn. Her foot has a complicated fracture, so the doctor says she has to wear it for at least another month.

Lily said, "Everyone is so wonderful, it's good to hear their stories about him. I had no idea he had so many friends."

"Me either," Merry said, "and I lived with him for the last four years."

"When he was with you, he was just with you, right?" I asked. He had been so present, so available.

"Yes, and all these people had the same experience with

him. I don't know where it came from, all that goodness. Maybe his mom." Lily looked over at her, standing nearby and talking to a group of anarchist bike messengers, one of whom was holding her hands and speaking sincerely, into her eyes.

"Lil, I forgot to tell you," Merry said, "my mom really wanted to come today but couldn't afford the ticket. She called the house and talked to Brix's mom on the phone this morning, and she wanted me to send you her love."

"Thanks. My mom wanted to come too. So did Brix's sister…she couldn't get away after taking all that time off when she was here last month."

"She would love this."

Lily nodded sadly. I wanted to take her away from all these people and lay her down to rest. But I knew she needed to be here with all of us, because we had all suffered a loss. Brix had helped people have better lives, often by fixing them up a bike, as he had for me. He'd been moving a lot of bikes through his workroom beneath the house, not charging much, just enough to keep doing it. He'd made people happy with his music too, always carrying his harmonica and breaking it out often, willing to be silly. And he'd been a mentor at the urban garden.

Now here Lily sat in her daisy crown and vintage black dress, her dirty bare foot tucked underneath her, surely the world's coolest widow. It seemed right to call her that, because even though she and Brix hadn't married and probably never would have, I knew that two people never loved each other as much as Lily loved Brix, and Brix loved Lily. It was inconceivable that she could go on without him, and yet here she was.

Someone above us opened a window, and his music poured out. Lily said, "Merry, you want to play a few Bogus

Basin songs? I know the guitar part."

Merry smiled and nodded, surprised but game, and Lily asked me to grab her banjo from Brix's bed. I went to get it, and Merry went into the house to get her guitar, hiking up the patchwork skirt I'd picked for her at the Naked Party.

I brought the banjo to Lily and went to sit with July, Terra, and Asha. Merry sat down on the blanket again, having turned the inside music down.

They started to strum together, a song Brix had written for Lily, called "My Lady." Lily smiled when she sang *"My lady, she licks me in the most private places / My lady likes to take me in the most public spaces."* The earrings she wore, long and beaded with tiny mirrors, reflected her out onto us.

They played a couple more of Merry and Brix's songs, and then I remembered the haiku I'd written for Brix and pulled it from my pocket nervously, then propped the gum wrapper in front of Lily and Merry on the blanket.

And then they sang my haiku, letting their instruments rest, their voices swirling perfectly around each other:

This moment is all
This sweet breath the universe
Our Brix lives in it

They sang it over and over, Merry's voice high and sweet, Lily's low and fierce. There was no sound in the yard but them reaching out for him.

They looked like they'd been doing it for years. Like there'd never been a Bogus Basin, or even a Lily and Brix— like it had been Lily and Merry all along.

August 25

Lily made a flag from the fabric from Brix's memorial. She sewed on all the photos that people had pinned up and attached the flannel to a long piece of driftwood. Out back, above the porch seat, there's a flagpole, and we're flying the flag there, at least until the rain starts. Claudia and Ingy didn't make it to Brix's memorial and were really sad that they missed it, but the flag makes them feel like they were part of it.

It reminds me of the old days, when a whole town would unite in caring for the family of the recently departed. It unites our house, brings the three floors together, in mourning. And in celebration. Letting our freak flag fly.

August 28

I hid in the herb closet today. My own little world. My world keeps reducing in size, like Russian dolls. From a country to an attic to a closet…

July and I had the house to ourselves. But we couldn't agree on what to make for fucking lunch of all things.

I said, "Pasta?"

She said, "No, I can't have any more carbs today."

I said, "Soup?"

She said, "I had soup for dinner last night."

And suddenly I couldn't take any more. I've been cooking for weeks for Lily, who would have every reason to be picky, but who has never once not wanted what I offered.

I lost my patience with July, but I didn't have the energy for a fight, so I just walked out of the kitchen. I didn't want to go up to the attic, where I knew she would just follow me, so when I saw the herb closet I went in and quietly closed the door behind me.

Being in the closet brought back my terrible hyperventilating in Nandi's closet. My hoodie baby. The parade of gruesome images, the beautiful and the ugly.

I sat against the wall, my head nestled in just under the bottom shelf. It felt like I was entombed. Pure quiet and darkness, for as long as I wanted. As long as was not too cruel. I figured July would assume I'd gone out.

I can't stop thinking about that moment on the porch at Brix's memorial, the hug I cut short with Lily because I worried what July would think behind me. Part of me turned off to July then, and it hasn't turned back on.

I don't want her taking me away from where I need to be. I need to be in the darkness.

It smelled like dirt in there, good and pure medicines of the earth. When I came out, July was gone.

September 2

July walked in on me Skyping with Sean today. She must have let herself in with her key, and I didn't hear her coming. Suddenly she was up here, and his head was on my computer screen. To make it worse, I whipped around guiltily. And then he saw her, he saw me turn around and act weird.

The whole thing was awful. I told him I had to go and clicked off.

I didn't know what to say. I didn't know where to start. I just sat there, immobile, looking at her. She was wearing the yellow T-shirt she got from the Naked Party, and her hair was doing the wave thing I love.

I was frozen, couldn't speak. I just looked at her, levelly, then away.

She turned around and went back down the stairs. I stood to follow her but when I got to the top of the attic steps she had already turned the corner and was gone. There were too many stairs between us for me to chase after her.

Fuck. Now what?

September 3

I just got this text from July:

I don't know who that guy is, or what you're keeping from me, but I can't do this anymore. I can't be with someone who won't talk to me.

I texted back:

I understand. You're right, it's not fair. It's better this way. I'm sorry.

I am so fucking good at walking away. But I had to.

The end is so fresh, it's hard to believe, like death. I have to keep running it through my mind in order to get it through to my bones.
   I keep rereading the texts. She didn't write back.
   It's over.

My hands are shaking. What did I do? I ruined this too?

Okay, breathe. First, just fucking breathe.

Now. Keep your mind away from the sweet memories. They are nothing but trouble. Do not think about July kissing you, gazing at you with her yellow eyes, fucking you from behind. Mind over matter. You can do this.

You need to help Lily through this time, and you need to deal with your own fucking loss. You can't do that with July. She needs way more than you can give her. You knew this was going to happen, and now it has. It's actually quite simple.

Probably half the couples in the world wouldn't be together now if they'd just been a little better at breakups. And you're not one of those people who needs a relationship. Now you won't have to be under the microscope all the time. You can be in touch with Sean without having to hide it.

He texted, to see what was up after I hung up on him, and I told him July and I broke up.

I took down our stupid bed fort. I put all the things she's given me into the suitcase under the altar with the rest of my old shit. I lit the sage Asha made me and carried it around the attic like I knew what I was doing. It's resting on a soy sauce bowl on the windowsill overlooking S.F., and now the air outside is sucking the smoke down toward the crack house, where they're now calling up to me.

I went to the window and called down, "What?"

They said, "What you got burnin' up there?"

"Sage," I said.

"Like, the spice?" one of them asked. A super skinny older Black woman in pink high-top sneakers. "Like, turkey dinner sage?"

"Yep," I said.

"What you doin' smokin' sage?" asked a Latino man with glasses, probably 50 or so.

I laughed. "Not smoking it. Burning it."

Four or five of them were squinting up at me, sweetly. They seemed concerned.

"It's supposed to clear out bad energy," I called down. "I just broke up with my girlfriend."

"Not the one next door?" the Black woman asked.

I couldn't believe it. I had no idea they knew anything about me. "Yeah. Her."

"Honey, you two look good together! You got to get her back."

I smiled, then gave a little wave, and stubbed out the sage.

September 12

I told Lily that July and I broke up, and she just nodded like she understood, didn't ask for more details. Maybe she knows I don't want to talk about it.

But she's been asking me questions about other stuff, and I feel like the least I can do is answer them. Sometimes I have a moment's hesitation, start up my old internal strategy session, but really, what's the harm? With all that's happened, my secrets are starting to seem pretty mild.

One thing leads to another leads to another…and I'm slowly being revealed. The truth is, it's a relief. The truth is a relief.

When I landed here, I was so afraid. I was running from my fear, and that made me even more afraid. Then I needed to maintain the lies, and that created even more fear, a lack of trust, like it was me against the world.

With July, it didn't feel safe to tell her the truth. I knew it would never be enough. When Lily asks me something, it's because she's really curious. Like today, she wanted to know more about the kids I taught. Her only selfish impulse is wanting a distraction, which I'm happy to give. She doesn't want to unravel me, she's busy keeping her own self tied together.

I told her about Sean too. That he's my ex, that he came back into my life recently. That we've known each other since we were kids but got together just before we moved to Japan. She nodded, taking this in, looking at me like she was considering whether to call me on my shit or just let it go.

Finally she said, "Oh, Nara. You sure do take a long time to open up." I let out a big breath I'd been holding in, and we both laughed. It feels so good not to be hiding from her anymore.

Some days we play gin rummy, or Scrabble. I tell her stories, or read to her, or we watch a movie. I'm still enjoying my Lily time. It doesn't matter that her light's gone out a little, she's still magic.

And she's getting better, I think. It's almost imperceptible, but I think she is. Having me take over basic life maintenance freed her up to do what she needs to do for herself. She needs good food, she needs greens and grains, and some sweet now and then, especially in the evening. She needs warmth, baths and flannel sheets and the soft blanket on the couch. She needs to write down what she's feeling and share it with her sister when they talk on the phone.

Some nights she needs me to sleep with her. She says it helps her not have nightmares, or not be as scared when she wakes from them.

When she needs air, and nature, I help her out back, slow and steady with her cast, step by step on the old wooden stairs. She sits out on the couch, meditating or reading, soaking up the Indian summer. I might bring her food, or tea. Ingy and Sharky might come to be with her, or Claudia often sits with her for hours. I try to take this time to do my own stuff, not watch her from the window.

She has almost no desire to go out into the rest of the world, like me when I first got here. The outside world was too much for me most days, as it is for Lily now. It's not what's needed. I can venture out for whatever she needs, or her friends can bring it.

We're getting high again—not a lot, but a little. It's fun, as long as we steer clear of darkness, toward distraction.

I'm trying valiantly to keep my mind from playing slides of Lexy and July fucking—under July's ocean ceiling, on their kitchen island, on the bathroom floor…Lexy on top, of course. They know I'm watching, and they're laughing at me.

How gay is that, having an ex-girlfriend next-door neighbor? Who lives with her ex-girlfriend. Perfect.

I'm afraid to go out back now. When I do, I want to look good, in case one of them sees me.

I was remembering the Naked Party the other day. It was only four months ago, but it feels like another story altogether.

FALL

September 22

6:33 a.m.

I just woke up crying from a dream of July. My body misses hers. It's so tempting, the thought of going to her, climbing into her window and curling myself around her sleeping body....

Breaking up feels like shit. And there's no way around it for me now, through the suck and the muck. So I keep myself busy with caring for Lil, cooking and cleaning…I try to avoid quiet moments to myself. I don't talk to my roommates about July, because I don't want anyone trying to change my mind. Terra started to try; I changed the subject.

But when I'm alone in the kitchen, sometimes the proximity to her is too much. I feel her presence behind me when I'm cooking and it hurts so bad I can't stop my tears from falling into the soup. I smoke on the porch with my back to her place now. I imagine her watching me from her room. Some days it rains; other days I can see the bay.

I feel like a stained-glass window, the pieces connected by the creation of a larger whole, but separate from one another and independent. Maybe from a distance my life looks whole, even beautiful. Maybe in time the lead between the pieces will melt away and all the me's will be integrated. I'm afraid that day is coming, afraid the lead is the glue that's been holding me together.

My intuition led me here, and now I know why. Yes, it was to meet July, to learn how to be with a woman, but it was also to catch Lily, to keep her from the abyss.

It feels like being a mother. Losing oneself in care for others. Finding a purpose there. It's satisfying, simple. This I can do, Lily's needs I can meet.

She's grateful, she shows me with her eyes. She thanks

me with the empty bowls and plates and mugs and with the life coming back to her face. Her laugh is a heavenly thank you that I crave—I'm a clown for her, some days, I find funny things and bring them to her. When she laughs, all is right in the world. I can forget my lost lover, I can forget my lost baby, and just focus on the sound of healing happening.

Because what is my grief compared to hers? Mine is nothing, laid out next to the deep pit of hers, like a tunnel to nowhere that never ends.

Until it does. I know Lily can get there, if anyone can. Her light has dimmed, but it's not all the way out. I keep fanning the flame. Without it she wouldn't be Lily, and I don't want to lose her too.

September 28

It's my mom's birthday. This makes me want to scream. Instead I bought her some hoops on Etsy.

I do all my screaming in my head. Butoh-style.

Face and hands painted with turmeric, black bob straightened. Black bodysuit and black lace bustle skirt, bare legs.

I am a lioness, and I grab the atmosphere around my head and pull it back so I can scream into the hole I've made. I sway to the vibration.

I hold my belly. I hold my arms, draw myself in. Circle my neck, side to side, my head falling deeper and deeper downward with each revolution until it reaches the floor.

And then I cut a circle below me with my rotating head, a pit, and start screaming into it with everything I have. Shoveling rage down, down, into the well.

The hoops are small, simple, gold. Straight from the seller, so no worry about the postmark. They'll probably end up in a drawer somewhere with all the other presents I've bought her for the last 30 years. All the unwanted trinkets, screaming together in the darkness.

October 8

Looking down at July's room, the palm tree is in the way, but her curtains are drawn anyway. I keep hoping to see, I don't know. Her. Looking up at me.

It's been a month, I guess the novelty of being single has worn off. I've now officially masturbated to thoughts of Lily, Asha, Terra, and Merry. Even Nandi. It's like a big elaborate porno production up in my brain, lots of costume changes and creative positioning. My fantasies are much more detailed than they need to be. Anything to avoid thinking of July.

Going downstairs and seeing one of them after just imagining them in that way is slightly awkward. I'm like *la-di-dah, doo-de-doo,* whistling and twiddling my thumbs, praying they don't somehow know.

I'm silent when I come, which ends up reminding me of July anyway. Her orgasms were quiet, but her body said it all, bucking against me, riding the good feeling, so goddamn sexy.

Sean and I chatted again today, on Facebook. He told me Patrick is teaching him to surf at the beach where we learned to swim. Those same waves that crashed us down when we were little—so many times, I thought I wasn't gonna make it back to the surface. I wanted to come visit and see him surf, but I was too afraid to ask.

Lying in bed just now, I heard the high wail of an orgasm, like the howl of a wolf on the wind. It came from next door, for sure. It didn't sound like any sound July would make, but it very well may have been caused by her.

She's one of my ghosts now.

When I went to close my curtains, when I looked down I caught a flash of July in her window. There, and then gone.

October 13

When Lily asked for a story last night, I decided to tell her. The big one. At least some of it. It just suddenly felt right.

I said, "I'll tell you the story of the thing I wanted most in the whole world."

Sean had hoped she would keep us together. I had hoped she would keep *me* together.

"It was not an easy pregnancy," I started.

Lily looked over at me, surprised, raised her eyebrows.

"I had terrible nausea, and was insanely emotional. The fatigue was crazy too. I would fall asleep at school, curled up with the kids at naptime. My boss thought I was so weird. But I was probably happier than I've ever been."

I thought I would stay that way, that she would make me happy finally. I thought she could save me from a life I didn't love. I just didn't realize I had these expectations until this moment.

It seems so delusional now, nothing but a setup.

"I went to a New Year's Eve party. In Japan the new year is the biggest holiday—the whole country shuts down for a few days after. A friend of my good friend Clara was having a party near me, and Clara couldn't make it, but said I should go. Sean was out of town, and I was tired of being alone.

"I rode my bike to the party, balancing some sweet red beans I had made, one of the traditional New Year's dishes. I wore my favorite dress, this long-sleeve, flowered baby-doll dress, over jeans. I wasn't showing yet. I had a little bump, but no more than I have now." I rested my hands on my belly and remembered how it had felt, having her in there.

Willow had been 22 weeks old. I couldn't bring myself

to say that out loud. Lily looked like I had felt when she told me about Brix, sitting in her bed. Not knowing what was around the corner but afraid of it, whatever it was.

"It was a relief to be around people who didn't know I was pregnant, if only for a night. At school my students loved to talk about the baby, and all the parents worried over me. At home, when Sean was there, he was constantly obsessing about her development.

"So that night, surrounded by these sweet Japanese kids who knew nothing about me, I felt like I could relax. I spoke Japanese without worrying how bad I sounded—they all praised me, of course. They welcomed me, even though they didn't know me, even though I was a foreigner. My friend's friend, the one who lived there, was this super sweet girl named Kyoko.

"They were playing this great Japanese hip-hop, which I'd never heard before, kind of trancey and with really good beats. I danced a little, just moving with the music, not worrying what I looked like.

"I didn't realize it at the time, but Kyoko kept refilling my sake glass, not knowing I was pregnant. So my one glass of sake that I was allowing myself—and it was good sake, very strong—turned into who knows how many. And it took a while to hit me."

I hadn't thought about this stuff in all these months, and man, it hurt. My stomach had felt hollow and sick. I asked Lily if I could have one of her Xanax, and she said of course. She told me they were in the drawer in her bedside table, which I already knew.

I took one, then took a big breath. "Someone suggested we walk to the beach, which was just a couple blocks away. They lived even closer than I did. On our walk I started to feel the sake.

"I don't remember much of the rest of the night. We ran down to the water. I wrote her name in the sand." I can still see it in my head, the tall, slanting letters leading one into the next. *Willow.*

"I had just found out that she was going to be a girl. I was so happy, Lil. I'd really wanted a girl. Walking back from the doctor's office, I passed a willow tree, and decided to name her Willow."

She said, "Beautiful name."

"Thanks. So anyway, that night, some of the kids I was with were surfers, and they stripped down and went in the ocean. It wasn't that cold, actually—I guess that's how I should have known I was wasted. I took my jeans off and went in too, in my dress. The moon was lighting up the ocean, shining on my new friends. They looked so happy.

"After a while somebody said it was almost midnight. A bunch of them decided to try to make it to the temple on the hill, to hear the temple bells ring in the new year. Kyoko and her boyfriend stayed, and when I got out they gave me a big towel. We saw a group of teenagers with a bonfire and joined them, warming up.

"After a while we heard the temple bells. In between, after each of the twelve gongs, the world was completely silent. They washed away everything that had come before.

"I don't remember how I got home, but I woke up in the middle of the night, terribly parched. I walked to the kitchen and poured myself a big glass of water, and the next thing I knew I was on the floor, and the water was spreading around me. I'd passed out, and I'd dropped the water glass, which broke. I lay there for a long time, afraid to move, my dress and hair soaked."

I paused, not knowing where to go from there.

"So what happened? What happened to the baby?"

But I couldn't do it. I told her it was late, she needed sleep.

I was afraid. I'm afraid what she'll think when she hears the whole story.

October 14

I rode my bike down to the bay today. I needed to get away from Lily, from the story. I left her a note and slipped out before she got up.

By the freeway I ran a red light and almost got hit by a Prius. The driver yelled at me, "Fucking stupid idiot!" and I nodded aggressively at her, agreeing.

I went down to where I threw up that weird morning. S.F. was covered in fog. Smelling the funk of the bay and hearing the squawk of the seagulls, all I wanted was someone to protect me, to keep me safe.

I went out to the end of the jetty, made my way down to the water, and sat on the rocks. I felt cold remembering Willow inside me, pulled my sweater around me. I have no proof that she ever existed.

I acted like a crazy person, lying, denying. There was so much good in Japan that I turned my back on too. I couldn't talk about the baby, and the baby was contained in Japan, so I couldn't talk about Japan. The kids, the people, the love, the beauty, I buried all of it when I left.

I held myself and rocked. I sat there for hours, thinking about my next move. There was a breeze over the bay, swirling my thoughts into spirals.

After a while I started to worry about Lily, feeling like I should go back and check on her. I hadn't brought my phone.

For the first time, I resented my obligation to her. I would have loved to feel that I could go to San Francisco, to Japan, if I wanted. When I get out of the house I feel how tied to it I've been. It's not enough.

I remembered one of the pictures from Brix's flag, of him sailing just out there in the bay. He was facing forward, in profile, like a masthead, his beard blowing in the wind.

October 16

Lily asked to hear the end of my story tonight. There was no more avoiding it. Asha and Terra were out, it was just the two of us on the couch after dinner. Toe to toe, drinking whiskey.

I'd never drunk whiskey before. It helped. I asked Lily for another one of her Xanax, and that helped too. I wasn't sure if she knew that there are only four left, and only a few more Oxys than that, but if she does she hasn't mentioned it.

Finally I felt ready. "I spent the rest of my New Year break, four days, sleeping. I was *so* tired, Lil. I would get up in the morning, make my tea, take it back to bed, and fall asleep again. My whole body was exhausted. I wanted to go see my doctor, to make sure Willow was okay after my fall. But the doctor's office was closed, everything was closed for the break.

"That Wednesday, school started back up, and I was happy to be with the kids again. They distracted me from my worry. I still wasn't feeling right and was planning to leave work early to go to the doctor."

Sean had been away, due back the following Monday, the day after I left Japan. But I didn't tell Lily this. Something about me having left him, and her being left by Brix…it was too much.

"After lunch, I sat on the rug to read to the kids. Toshi climbed in my lap, and I was going to read them Dr. Seuss's *Sleep Book,* to get them ready for naptime.

"I moved Toshi out of my lap and started to reach for the book, and then all of a sudden my abdomen started cramping, and suddenly I was doubled over in pain, on my hands and knees.

"I felt a terrible dripping start down my legs. I was

wearing that same damn babydoll dress but no jeans this time, and suddenly it was…she was…just pouring out of me." I gagged, and Lily looked alarmed.

I stared at her, sitting across from me, but just like when she looked at me and saw desert, I looked at her and saw blood.

I took a sip of my whiskey. I really didn't want to keep going. I knew she could take the horror of what happened next, with all of her pediatric training, but I didn't know if I could.

I tasted something terrible in the back of my throat. The whiskey. The shame.

I hadn't even understood what a big role shame had played in my suppression of all of this. I didn't want to be someone to whom such horrid things had happened. Someone who had singlehandedly traumatized several small humans. But also, someone who had suffered such indignity, so publicly, in a country that couldn't tolerate it. In Japan, such intimate, private bodily functions, not to mention such trauma, only ever happened behind closed doors.

"The blood streamed out of me forcefully, past my underwear, all over the rainbow-shaped rug where the kids had been sitting, crisscross applesauce, waiting for a story.

"Thick, clotted blood. There was so much blood, Lily. It was almost black."

I felt sick, remembering. I thought I might pass out.

I rested my head against my knees, pulling my legs tightly into me. I couldn't believe I was telling another human, that meant it had happened. It was real.

I needed to not back away this time.

I continued, with my eyes closed, remembering, "My students jumped up and away from me."

I whispered, "Some of them had gotten splattered."

Lily reached out and took hold of both of my ankles, and it helped, grounding me in the room. When I opened my eyes I found her waiting there, concern in her eyes.

I exhaled. "All the kids were huddled in a corner, across the room. Probably my boss had corralled them there, but I can't see her, only them."

Their faces were like little moons. Very pale and very afraid. I've done everything I could since then to avoid seeing those faces again. The running. The hiding. From them.

I took a deep breath, and Lily nodded.

"My boss took the kids to the downstairs classroom, and she must have called an ambulance from her cell. I rocked through the pain, in child's pose. The cramps were insane."

Through my terror, I remember thinking that it was all over. Me and Sean, my conflict about being with someone I wasn't really attracted to. My worries about the kind of mother I would be, about whether Willow would be healthy... All of those unknowns were gone, because I knew that I had lost her.

I told Lily, "My school slippers were soaked with her." Even as she blanched, I continued, "I don't remember taking them off. Now that I think about it, they sent me home in little hospital booties. What shoes did I wear to school that day?"

It was a stupid mystery, but oddly compelling. I tried to remember but could not.

I never went back up to that classroom after they took me away on the stretcher, down the walking path.

There were other things of mine too up there, I remembered now. All kinds of toys and knickknacks I had bought all over Japan and decorated our classroom with. Stuffies of Miyazaki characters and Rilakkuma. And so many kids' books.

Lily asked quietly, "What happened at the hospital?"

"My memories are pretty vague. They…removed the rest of her. They gave me something that knocked me out."

I remember now that I woke up alone and confused—by the drugs, by the language, the bright lights. I had lost her, in this violent way, and no one spoke to me about depression.

I lost her, and then I almost lost myself, after that. I had wanted to, had wanted to sink into the sea. To take the whole bottle of Vicodin and swim away with her.

I didn't mention to Lily how much pain I was in those first couple days, how vulnerable I felt, alone and worried something else would happen. I hadn't understood a lot of what the doctor explained about after-care but they were very worried about how much blood I had lost. I couldn't deal with Lily's judgment around how irresponsible I had been with my health.

So I downplayed the rest. I had split open my insides far enough. I told Lily, "I had only felt her in me once, a week earlier. Not even a kick—just a flutter. So when she was gone it wasn't so different."

This of course was not true. Losing Willow left me alone like I'd never been alone.

After telling Lily, I wanted to be alone again. I came up here to write this down.

I feel numb, like I did then. The Xanax feels like the Vicodin did.

October 20

A bunch of Lily's friends, and Brix's, came over tonight for a potluck in the backyard. I know now that Lily is going to get through this.

Terra told me she and Asha are getting their own place. It's sad that they're moving out, but Asha and I aren't talking much so I guess it will be better. I wished they were here tonight, though. I felt very alone, without them, without July, Lily busy with everyone else. I've been feeling miserable since remembering Willow.

I sat on the back steps and looked over at Ingy and Claudia, sitting and holding hands on the picnic bench, and the words *I will never have that* came out of nowhere and knocked the wind out of me.

I rested my head on my knees and wrapped my arms around my legs, holding myself tight. The heartbreak heated up my chest and I moved my head from side to side, fighting it.

The loss of Brix, who she adored, freaked Ingy out. I wasn't as available as I had been, and of course neither was Lily, or Asha…so Ingy turned to her mom, which was the best place for her. Claudia also loved Brix—they'd been very close, and losing him reminded Claudia how easily her daughter could be snatched away.

She had looked like a seahorse when I saw her on that last ultrasound, when I found out she was a girl. I loved to think of her that way, my little seahorse swimming around inside me.

I don't think July could have come with me here, to this part of my healing. Or anyway, I don't think I could have gotten here with her witnessing. I was too afraid to let her see all the blood and guts.

I've started sleeping mostly in my room again, so I'm closer to July's room, and it's harder not to think about her, wonder what she's doing in there. My eyes wander down to her window when I'm sitting at my desk, like now, but I've never seen her, other than that one flash. She always did keep her curtains drawn.

Caring for the yard has been no one's priority lately, and it's grown with a wildness that feels appropriate. I turned my head to the side and watched Sharky rooting around through the weeds and wildflowers, hidden except for his wagging tail. I looked over at Lily, in conversation with some bearded guy who will never be Brix, and closed my eyes, letting the urge to save her come and go.

A few minutes later I heard a creak from the stairs and felt an arm around me. I turned my head and looked up into Lily's face as she settled in beside me. "You okay?"

"Just tired."

She nodded and said, "We're talking about going to New Orleans for Day of the Dead next month—by then my cast should be off. A lot of Brix's friends live there. You should come, if you want."

"New Orleans, that's where July lived last," I said.

"Oh, yeah—I saw July, out front, a little while ago. I think she was coming home, but she looked a little lost. I gave her a hug, and she seemed surprised. She started to cry and told me she was sorry about Brix, and that her brother died when she was 16. Did you know that?"

"Yes," I said.

"Well, she said Brix's death triggered some hard stuff for her from that time. She felt really bad that she wasn't able to be a support to me. I told her not to worry about it, and that she should come in. But she didn't."

We were silent for a minute.

"You should go talk to her," she said.

"Yes," I said, but my body wouldn't move.

I talked to Ingy at the potluck about Halloween. It's her favorite holiday too. She wants to show me Russell Street in Berkeley, which they close to traffic. Tons of people come out and the houses are all dramatically decorated.

I told her she should be Princess Mononoke, and she said I should be her white wolf mama, Moro. I'm gonna help her put together a costume—Lily said I can use her sewing machine. It'll be good to have a project.

Ingy's hair is already perfect, and she has a black skirt and a white tank top that we can rough up. The big thing will be making a cape. And some sort of costume for me. We're going to a big fabric store on Shattuck tomorrow to see if they have white fake fur. Ingy has a long stick she'll carve into a spear. And she may even be able to make her mask in art class, with papier-mâché.

I'm excited, my first real Halloween in five years. The parties we had with the kids in Japan don't count. For me, coming up with with the otherworldly gay phenomenon of the Castro District in college, Halloween is all about being outside, going a little wild, becoming something else for a night.

October 24

Asha and Terra moved out today. It's what I dreamed of when I first moved in, being alone with Lily, but now of course I know it's not really what I want.

So we went to Muir Beach for the day. I didn't want Lily to have to witness losing Asha and Terra too, and I didn't want to see them go either…

We decided, on our drive to the beach, to wait a little while to find a new roommate—rent is paid through the end of the month. After that, money's tight for me, but Brix's mom gave Lily what was in Brix's savings and checking accounts, and Lily wants to use it to cover the room until she can figure out where to put all of his stuff.

It's been good not having a job during this time when Lily needed help, and she's supporting me too by paying Asha's rent. Buys us a little time and keeps costs low until I can get it together to find paying work.

Since some of the living room furniture was Asha's, there's more room for us to spread out in there now too. It was good to come home and have them be gone, the room empty for us to move Brix's stuff into. I don't have to wonder every time I pass by Asha's room if she's in there. Lily can cook in the mornings without inciting Asha's rage.

At the beach, we climbed carefully to the top of the same big rock I'd climbed on Willow's due date, wishing for Freeda to come and take me to her. I gave Lily a push or a pull when she needed it. When we got up there, we sat on the edge and let our legs dangle, her right leg all sandy in its cast.

She threw some of Brix's ashes into the sea, and we watched him become ocean. When we climbed down it was me helping her, one slow step at a time.

I made us a fire. Her first since the one in the desert, she said. The last time Brix had been up and alive.

San Francisco, just around the corner, was blocked by large cliffs on both sides. Out in front of us was nothing but Japan.

I told Lily about my life there. I painted pictures of the beach and the food shacks, of Daibutsu and the temples. Of the preschool, and the kids. The foot paths that ran in front of my house and all through the city, like a language you had to learn in order to find your way through, to emerge roughly where you hoped to.

"Last December," I told her, "it snowed. I woke up early in the morning and saw the snow falling through our big front window. I put on warm clothes and started down the path in front of our house, which led all the way to the beach. White all around me, covering everything, like a fresh new world. It was completely silent, nothing but the sound of my boots crunching. I sang to Willow as I walked."

"Wait. Hold on." She was staring at me over the shivering flame. "It was this January you lost her? Like, right before you moved in?"

I froze. I hadn't planned to tell her, but I've stopped micromanaging what comes out of my mouth and I forgot. I nodded.

"I didn't understand that," she said. "How soon after the miscarriage did you leave Japan?"

"A few days," I said quietly.

"Have you seen a doctor since it happened?"

I shook my head.

"Nara, what the hell! You need to take care of yourself."

"I don't have insurance," I said lamely.

"Hello, we have a million free clinics in the Bay Area.

There's one in Fruitvale I used to volunteer at. Shit, even I could have checked you, it'd be better than nothing. Why would you hide that from us?"

I shook my head, looked out at the ocean.

"Am I the only person who knows about the baby?"

"You're the only one here. Yes." I could feel my heart starting to clench up.

"You never told July? Or Asha?"

"No." I shook my head again, and looked over at her. We stared each other down for a moment, and then I got up. I put my hood on and walked down to the water. I rolled up my pants and went in up to my knees. The cold was so satisfying. Soon I'd be numb.

I wanted a Xanax. Felt my back pockets, where I sometimes stashed one, but no luck. I started getting defensive, thinking, *It was the only way I could manage it, alone. To forget it for a while was the only way I could survive it.*

It felt that way at the time. Turns out I'm stronger than I thought.

I looked down the beach to where I carved Willow's name in the sand, in my wet pants, on her due date. Even that me felt so far away.

My whole body turned cold to Lily. From that cold place it felt true: that I don't need anyone. That I don't have to feel anything I don't want to feel.

Eventually the cold turned to numb and I welcomed it. How wonderful, to not feel anything. How beautiful and calm, the gray fog that came in and covered it all.

I did not want to go back up to Lily. I did not want to have to talk about it anymore. She couldn't go down to the water without me, so it was mean of me to stay away, a tiny power trip. Maybe I was tired of taking care of her.

The coldness had just turned on in me, it hadn't felt like

I had a choice. But then I remembered that I did have a choice, there was another way. It was just a glimmer, but it was enough to pull me back to the shore.

I came out of the ocean and sat on the sand, let the feeling come back into my legs. I imagined the creatures in the ocean. Their world would be dark soon. I imagined Brix out there, his ashes part of them now. He could find my little seahorse, look out for her.

I started to shake, then, thinking of her. How could I ever have denied her existence, even for a second? Had I really been too embarrassed to honor her short life?

I saw a sand pail left behind and scooped some seawater in it to take back to Lily. When I got to the blanket she was lying on her back, looking at the stars arriving in the sky.

"Brought you some ocean," I said, setting the bucket in the sand. "Sorry I was gone so long."

She looked over at me.

I put another log on the fire. "I'm sorry I didn't tell you sooner."

"I just wish I could have helped you through it."

"You did, though. I needed to forget for a while."

"Okay, I get that."

The sunset came in fierce, like it was trying to match the fire's glory. It's setting early now, around 6:30.

And then she said, "There's something I haven't told you. I don't like to talk about it. But it doesn't feel right, keeping it from you now."

Her cheeks had salt tracks on them, lit by the fire.

"I had an abortion, two years ago, when Brix and I were just getting together. I really wanted the baby, and he didn't. We almost broke up because of it." She started crying again, and I moved down to the blanket and sat holding her forearm awkwardly. "It was awful, though I'm sure nothing compared to what you went through. I can understand why you don't want to talk about it."

"Thank you for telling me."

She took a deep breath. "And—I do want a baby. It wasn't right then because Brix would have had to want it too. Parenting is so hard, I feel like everyone has to be 100 percent. And now I can find someone to do that with me." She said it quietly, then looked over at me, chest hiccupping, eyes spilling over.

"He would want you to have that."

"Tell me the rest of your snow story," she said, looking up again.

I lay down next to her. "So as I walked to the beach in the snow, it was early and no one else was out. It was a world all our own, me and Willow. And that morning I was singing this song, to Willow:

The more it snows, tiddly pum, the more it goes, tiddly pum, the more it goes on snowing."

Lily said, "I know that song. From *The House at Pooh Corner.*"

"I had been reading it to my students, and to Willow, inside me. So that morning in the snow, it was like you and Brix on the moon. Me and Willow in the snow. It was so amazing, to be alone but not feel alone, because she was with me. I marched and sang.

"And then when we reached the beach, it was covered in snow. I couldn't believe it when I saw it, as if it was a dream. I walked down into it, and it was like walking on a cloud. My footsteps were the first, and they fell through to the sand, each one making a hole like four feet deep.

"It seemed a shame to mess it up, so I didn't go far. I just stood there, up to my hips in snow, and looked out at the snow falling on the ocean."

My girl and I had that.

Lily was quiet for a minute. Then she said, "When I was a kid we used to go sledding every day after school." She grew up in Michigan, with a sister and a lot of friends, so different from my quiet only-childhood. "Brix and I always made sure to get up to Tahoe a few times every winter. He always wanted to take me to Bogus Basin, in Boise. He and Merry snowboarded there in high school—that's where their band name comes from."

"Let's go. As soon as there's snow," I said.

I fed the fire, and she watched it. We ate the minestrone I'd brought.

Then we were the last ones on the beach. Like orphans stranded on the shore.

I lay down on my back, looked for some familiar constellation. "Is Brix up there?" I asked her, the question surprising me. I wanted to know if she still felt him, if she knew where he might be. I'm trying to understand it for myself. Where did he and Willow go?

"He is for me," she said. "He knew the stars really well. We did this every night we were out in the desert, just watched the show. He taught me so much about the stars. So I feel him when I look at them. He could be a star, he could be gazing down at us. He could be the muzzle of Ursa Major." She pointed out the constellation. "It's 138 times brighter than the sun."

"Sounds like him to me."

"I think he's at peace," she said after a pause. "For a while, I felt him around, like he didn't want to leave me. I spoke to him. I felt connected to him, still." She closed her eyes. "It was terrible, to feel him so close and not be able to touch or see him. But I was also glad he wasn't totally gone.

"Now he's gone," she said. "And why couldn't he live in the stars? He would love that.

"We talked a lot about reincarnation. He understood it, so in that way I think he was ready for death. He knew what was happening. He may have fought against leaving me, but whatever he's become, I think he's fully that, now. I have no idea what form he took, but I'll be looking for him for the rest of my life."

October 25

Earthquake off the coast of Indonesia, 7.7, started a tsunami. Hundreds dead and without homes.

Some butoh for the dead. Gray Depeche Mode T-shirt and gray lace underwear, the rest of my naked body painted gray. Sinking to the floor in a death spiral, only to be yanked back up just before falling, pulled upward by flowered ribbons trussing my forearms, cream silk with roses down the middle. Just as I almost reach my death I'm again and again pulled up and out, back to standing.

I fall back, and the ribbons catch me, make a cradle, a hammock I release myself to.

Underneath me, the stage shakes.

October 29

Lily left for New Orleans a couple days ago. I've been letting myself fall apart a little, sleeping a lot, taking a bath every day. Lily made me some herbal bath salts that are supposed to be restorative.

Since I have the house to myself, I've been writing downstairs. At the kitchen table, or on the couch. No more closet for me—I'm expanding to fill the whole house. Sometimes I even open the curtains.

I don't care if July sees me now. Before, I felt a little guilty, that I had Lily, that I was enjoying myself now and then. Now I'm just alone, and I kind of want her to see that.

The most you can ask is to be able to make a home with people you love. Our home is quiet now, with everyone gone, but it's still the first real home I've ever had.

October 31

Ingy and I had a fun Halloween. It was good to get out of the house. We saw some amazing costumes. Russell Street is like a miniature version of what the Castro used to be.

Ingy and I looked pretty fabulous too, if I say so myself. Her white fur cape turned out great, and she attached the papier-mâché mask she made and wore it over her face for most of the night. She was as fierce as Princess Mononoke herself, never breaking character.

For my part, as the wolf goddess Moro, I added furry white wolf ears and whiskers to the hood of a nubby white sweatshirt, and a tail in the back. I drew tribal markings on my forehead and cheeks to match Ingy's, wore white jeans of Lily's, and squeezed my feet into some white combat boots of Ingy's.

We didn't do much trick-or-treating. We saw some of Ingy's friends and hung out with them a bit, but Ingy didn't leave my side, embodying San's devotion to her wolf mama. She sensed my sadness, and she was sad too. It was an appropriately somber costume for two people grieving. In the movie I don't think San cracks a smile once—she's grieving too, for the forest.

But as we rode home, Ingy's cape flying out behind her, I felt the wildness of being out in the night, in the wind, and couldn't help but give a little howl.

The wolf princess howled right back.

November 2

Lily had asked all of Brix's friends to take five minutes of silence, starting at 7 p.m. today, the Day of the Dead. In this way we could be with her, in New Orleans, and with Brix.

I was boiling eggs, from Brix's chickens, to keep them from going bad since it's just me eating them this week. I looked up at the kitchen clock just as its hands reached 7.

I took the eggs from the boiling water and placed them in a bowl of cold water. One of them had cracked and some of its white was trailing behind like a ghost.

I went into the living room and sat at the altar we made for Brix, lit the candles there. Staring at his image, I focused on sending his spirit strength.

I cried out at the thought, still unfathomable, that he's not coming back.

Grief is a perpetual state of disbelief. If someone you love has left this world, how can you gracefully, gratefully stay in it? Isn't there always the desire to follow them wherever they've gone? How do we figure out where they went? How do we get there?

I focused on Brix's face—the big beard, the serious eyes—and thought of the dozens of other souls doing the same around the world, wondered if any of them had gotten any further in accepting his nonexistence. As much as I believe in reincarnation in theory, I couldn't shake the feeling that Brix was watching me—and if he was here in the living room with me, how could he be off cruising the Grand Canyon, or up there in the stars?

The Latin Americans celebrating their dead today think they're more likely to show up if we offer sweets, skeleton-shaped breads, marigolds. Before Lily left for New Orleans, we culled the giant altar from his memorial into this smaller one on our coffee table, decorated with photos and mementos of Brix. Lily's going to build some of the offerings people left into the walls of the cob house, and she took some with her to New Orleans too, for his friends there.

I've been keeping the marigolds fresh. I built a perch, a whiskey box with a scarf over it, for the little deer I bought for Willow at the antique store in Kamakura. I imagined Willow getting on the deer's back and riding away. I put the dove feather that I took from Lily's room, the one Brix gave her, on the perch with the deer.

Through my tears the candles bloomed into flowers of light. I replaced one that had burned away. The photo that always got me was that one of him on the sailboat in the bay, looking ahead, looking peaceful, like he knew what was coming. He died in peace, in his sleep, with Lily by his side. Maybe it was what he wanted.

I closed my eyes and imagined him there on the boat, and in my mind he had his drums set up on the deck, under the sun. I was with him, dancing butoh for his death, which we could see on the horizon. I got more time with him.

We celebrated with the wind and the water, the boat moving us swiftly in a limbo between Oakland and S.F., between life and death. Brix played the drums with a wildness I hadn't seen in him before, and I moved to them with the same ferocity, with everything I had.

When you've lost someone close to you, you become part of a tribe, a very tough tribe who's known the worst pain and survived it. Today was our day. I was soothed by the thought that we were all together in spirit, mourning all over the world.

Then, just as I had remembered to be with Brix at 7, I

recalled that tonight was the Día de los Muertos parade in the Mission. It was like something outside of me wanted me there.

I walked quickly to Ashby BART, arrived just as the S.F. train was pulling into the station and floated onto it. It was my first time going into the city by myself since I've been back, but again where to go, what to do was in my bones. As we got closer to the Mission, more and more human skeletons boarded. I wished I'd thought to bring Brix's flag. When they got off at 16th/Mission I followed them. We all walked together, collecting mourners as we went, until we caught up with the parade.

Many people carried candles for lost ones. Almost everyone was dressed as the dead, their costumes even more glorious than the ones I'd seen on Halloween. A pale face, dark rings around the eyes, a crosshatched mouth. Hearts and flowers and spider webs on the forehead and cheeks. Every one different from the others, and yet so alike that they looked like one big dead family.

The mood was solemn, but celebratory. I found a spot in the middle of the procession and walked through the Mission with the hundreds of others, feeling held. I happened to be wearing a black hoodie, and I pulled the hood over my head, my bangs hanging over my eyes.

At every street corner, the procession stopped and the Aztec dancers danced for the dead. In their giant, spectacular headdresses, adorned with the skulls and feathers of animals, they pressed their bare feet to the ground, stomping out their sorrow. Calling their lost ones back. Forward and backward, around and around, up and down, like magnificent creatures, their feathers tickling our faces.

Sage filled my head, the beat of the drums steadied me. I marveled at this place, this wonderful place, this place I had missed so deeply. I felt blessed, by the glitter, the candles, the sage. I closed my eyes, and let it all fall down on me.

I moved with the crowd, continuing my butoh dance in my head, and it was close as I could get to being with Brix and Willow—in between, neither here nor there. I grew candles on the ends of my hands and I raised the flames high, around and around in circles above me. I shook my head, *No, no, no.*

I fell back into the drum circle that had formed behind me, and I moved with the *pum, pum, pum, pum.* My head moved up and down with the tom, *Yes, yes, yes.* I followed the dancers, stomping my feet into the ground. All my resistance emptied away, and I cried, for freedom and for being alive.

I looked out at the wild skeleton posse surrounding me and knew I was one of them. We were united by loss, and love, by this beautiful place…the toddler with tears running down his face, bouncing on his dad's shoulders…the old man marching to the beat and holding a light bulb that was, inexplicably, lit…the many same-sex couples looking sharp and serious, holding hands…the Aztecs whooping as they danced their formal, ancient rituals of remembrance.

Mine was about letting go. As I let my body go—let it know what to do and do it—I thought maybe I could let go too of Willow, and of Brix, and of everything I had been holding in since I arrived.

I shook it all out of me, and as I looked around I saw the smiles of the dead in the faces of strangers.

I held my stomach, that sacred place that once housed a human, I held tight, and then I let go, I let her go, releasing Willow to the other spirits floating above our heads, darting in and out like hummingbirds.

November 5

Sean and I Skyped today. He wanted to show me all the stuff he has of mine so I can tell him what to do with it.

So weird, I was just wondering about the shoes I wore the morning of the miscarriage—Sean has them. Haruka gave them to him before he left. My black suede boots. I'd worn them with the damn babydoll dress the day we went back to school, the day I miscarried. I remember I'd felt hopeful that morning, that everything was okay.

He also has all of my stuffed animals and toys, and a ton of mail—Haruka is sending him all our mail every couple weeks, plus everything that came before he left. I asked him to send the mail but hold on to the boots and other stuff of mine he brought from Japan. His brother has room in his garage so it's not a problem.

I saw his brother passing by behind him and I said, "Hey, Patrick."

He said, "Hey, Sara. Or should I say *Nara*." He pronounced my name like it was the most pretentious thing on Earth.

"You can call me whatever you want, Patrick."

"Wow, thanks." He rolled his eyes at me and walked away.

"He'll come around," Sean said.

"Don't count on it," Patrick yelled back.

"I'm not worried," I told Sean. "I don't have to live with him."

We were quiet then, looking at each other shyly.

"You're getting buff, dude," I told him.

"Strength training." He smiled.

"Caught any waves yet?"

"I did, actually. I got up briefly the other day."

"Wow, that must feel so good."

"It does. It's amazing being out there. We see seals and dolphins all the time."

I paused. "I never told you this, but that last ultrasound, when I found out Willow was a girl, she totally looked like a seahorse."

"You left it on the fridge. I thought the same thing when I saw it."

"Yeah?" I smiled. "I always imagine her out there swimming in the ocean." I paused. "Maybe when you're surfing, she'll be out there with you."

My eyes filled up with tears and his did too. Both of us trying to protect the other from our emotion. Once we start, it feels like we'll never be able to stop.

He cleared his throat quietly and said, "She will."

"Thanks, buddy. Better say bye now."

"Yep. Take care." And then he pressed the hang-up button and was gone.

November 10

I finally realized today why the Japanese doctor at the hospital told me Willow was stillborn. He said "steer-boln," and for the longest time I couldn't understand what he meant, through the drugs and the language barrier it seemed like some bad joke, him and the nurse both saying it until finally I understood.

After 20 weeks a miscarried baby is termed a stillborn. I finally understand why was he going to such great lengths to get me to understand this.

It was to explain why my sadness would be so deep.

She was 22 weeks old. She was a real baby, the size of a banana, with eyebrows and eyelids and a tongue. With a tiny but fully formed womb.

And I may have killed her, with my drinking, with my fall.

I know there are many things that could have caused her death. The Internet has confirmed the multitude of reasons miscarriage can occur. But it doesn't matter. I didn't deserve her, if I could have forgotten her, even for a day, a few hours, a moment.

Because as deeply as I wanted her, as wholesomely as I wanted her, I know now that I also wanted her to save me, from my terrible aloneness. And now I see that I have saved myself, and this is the way it had to go. It would not have been fair to have used her, in this or any less than loving way. That, I would not have been able to forgive myself for.

Maybe somehow she knew the timing wasn't right. Or if not her then the ocean that saw me writing her name in the sand in the last moments of last year and said, *No, not now, not yet,* and pulled her essence from me, to ride the waves forever.

And then days later, when the rest of her was pulled from me in the classroom, as horrible and humiliating as it was to have all my students witness that…maybe that had to go that way too. I could never have left those kids, otherwise.

November 13

I just looked down and, through the palm tree, saw Lily driving away in Brix's truck. It's a dark blue pickup. She looks so tough and perfect in it. Farm girl at heart, soaking up the last of the boy, her curls unraveling. Since she has his truck she's selling me her Subaru.

She's been spending most of her time at Merry's, sleeping in the cob house, since she got back from New Orleans. Now that her cast is off she can get up and down the stairs there.

Her foot is mostly healed. Who knows if she'll ever be healed emotionally, but even wrecked she's more stable than anyone I know. She's going to finish her last semester of nursing school in the spring, and live in the cob house.

I haven't seen her much, but she seems distant. I'm afraid maybe she's mad at me because she saw that the feather's back, on Brix's altar, and she knows I must have taken it. Or she could be mad about the missing pills. I put a little note in each of the pill bottles saying I'm sorry they're almost gone and I like them too much for her to leave them here with me. The next time I checked they were gone.

She also could be mad about my lying, not telling them about the miscarriage, about Sean. We never talked about it after the beach.

Regardless, I know we are going to be okay. I finally figured out what Lily has represented for me. It's taken me all this time to figure it out because I've never felt it before.

Mothering. Getting to care for her. I needed to do that for someone, after I lost my chance with Willow.

And then, having someone to tell my story to. Someone who would be there for me like a mama would, to hear me clearly and not take it personally.

Her stuff is still here, and Brix's stuff is in Asha's room. The thought of looking for new roommates is too overwhelming right now, and rent is paid through the end of the year. The one thing I know for sure is that I don't want to leave this house.

November 18

I just got the craziest email from Asha. Copied and pasted, here it is.

Hey Nara,

Do you remember when we held hands on the train? Maybe it wasn't that big a deal to you, but it was the first time I held hands with a woman. It was a big deal to me.

I wanted to hold you, after that. I wanted to hold your secrets. I wanted to help you. But next thing I knew, you were isolating in the attic. I knew you didn't trust me, and it hurt.

And then you completely engineered me and Terra getting together—maybe to protect yourself from my interest? I know you thought I wanted her, but what I wanted was you. You were so funny at the Naked Party, trying to dress us up. But after seeing you naked, and flirting with July, I had to turn away. I knew you'd never look at me the way you looked at her.

So I turned to Terra instead. And of course I love her. But it was hard for me to get to this place, with you around. I'm sorry, but that's why I had to leave. I know that left you to care for Lily and I regret it.

Thank you for taking care of her. I'm sorry I wasn't strong enough to help, to be there for my dear friend in her deep need. I owe her an apology as well.

But losing Brix really messed me up, and when I saw the love you gave to Lily, I felt like I needed it too. But of course you couldn't give it to me—you were avoiding me, we both had girlfriends. Anyway, I didn't deserve it, because I didn't lose him like Lily did.

I was concerned about you lying to the others, but I knew it was nothing big. I know you. I heard that you and July broke up, and I was sorry to hear it. That's why I finally felt I could tell you this.

Terra and I are in it for the long haul, so it felt important to be clear about my feelings for you. They are separate from me and her.

I love you, Nara. I love your ability to be open, to give. Because I still don't know what you were coming from in Japan, but I know it must have been bad. And yet you got here and immediately opened up to us. Maybe you didn't tell us everything, but you opened yourself and that blew my mind. Because every bad thing I have experienced in my life has shut me down a little more.

I'm sorry to burden you with this now. But you were my first crush on a woman, and there's something precious there that I don't want to lose, despite everything else that happened. I don't want to keep it a secret anymore. It's just love.

You showed me what it could be like. It helped me so much, you telling me about Dani and Ai. I wanted all of that with you. I just didn't know how to ask. I was afraid you wouldn't feel the same, afraid of messing things up in the house.

My outer response to the softening happening in me was to harden. I wanted to be sweet and soft with you, but I didn't know how.

I hope that you will trust me with your secrets someday. I no longer want something romantic with you, but I really hope that we can be close again someday. I don't think I'm ready for that yet, but of course we will see each other around, and I hope it'll be okay. You know Terra and I are planning to have a baby together. I hope you'll be part of our baby's life.

Let's give it some time. Maybe we can stay in touch by email? Or if you need anything, please feel free to text me. Maybe I can offer you some support, something you are needing. I hope that's in our future.

All love,

Asha

I just read it again. All that time I was wondering about her, wanting more, she was too.… All that time I thought she was mad at me, it was really just love.

I feel so much lighter now, knowing she doesn't hate me. She loves me! She thinks I'm a good person.

It feels like I'm whole again. All this time, I didn't even let myself miss her. Just like with Willow, my students, Moony, Sean…I turned my back on Asha too, on our friendship. I made myself not care, because it hurt too much to care. I thought her coldness was a punishment for my secrets.

God, the wasted time, the wasted energy! We missed out on being there for each other as friends, through the stress of our new relationships, through Brix's death.…

But better late than never. I feel like writing her back right now, and saying, Yay! Let's be friends again. Let's be close like we were. None of the other stuff matters.

That even through all my bullshit, even with everything I was hiding, Asha loved me like that—it makes me feel like a whole human being.

But I'm going to wait a little while before I write her back. I feel like all the excitement in me could be dangerous for her right now, and dangerous for me too. All the sweetness and relief could make those romantic feelings come back. More than anything, I don't want to mess things up again.

And like her, I don't want to say anything less than the truth. No more lies.

I can wait, and just sit with the satisfaction of having another piece of the puzzle in place. My life is starting to make sense, I can almost see the design now. Something brighter and darker than your standard flat landscape. Something interesting, at least.

November 25

We had a vegan Thanksgiving tonight at Merry's. The huge chandelier was turned down low and candles stretched the length of the dining table, which was made from two picnic benches by Brix and Merry. The chairs around it are all different, found and refinished by Merry, who does this for a living. I sat in a rose-colored chair with a wide circle seat and magenta cushion. I chose it because it matched the blackberry peonies in the center of the table, which were so beautiful it was hard to believe they were real.

I love their weight, their heaviness. Their slowness to open, taking their sweet time.

The chair next to me, at the head, we left empty. For you know who, in case he came. Green and yellow satin, his throne. I liked imagining him there, laughing and pushing the peonies aside so he could see Lily at the other end.

I made vegan mashed potatoes, mushroom gravy, pumpkin pie. All stuff from our CSA, since I'm so broke. I checked my bank account today, and I have $64 left. Rent and bills are paid and between the CSA and Arizmendi I have more food than I can eat on my own, so I just keep telling myself that it's gonna be okay.

Claudia made empanadas, four different kinds, to try out on us. She's thinking of starting an empanada shop. Merry made a yummy nut loaf, and Lily made green beans, sweet potatoes, and a rainbow salad. Ingy made a plum crumble with the plums from our yard.

Asha and Terra are in Chicago, introducing Terra to Asha's parents. I wonder if they would have come if they'd been here. Asha might be shy around me for a while. I emailed her back to say I got her message and will respond soon. I'm still writing what I want to say in my head.

After dinner we made a fire in their living room. Lily and Merry settled into the couch and played some old songs, made up some new ones. We drank champagne, and Ingy and Claudia and I lay on the floor and played poker, our chips these beautiful old beads and buttons that Merry keeps in a goldfish bowl.

They are the best family I've ever had. Even with the pain we've all battled through this year—like moving through a terrible storm, the ice and snow threatening to take you down if you don't keep moving against it—the love in that room was bright and alive.

I remembered my dream of the bamboo forest and the spirits I saw in that strong light from above. I thought, *Spirits are probably always around, it's just that only once in a while is the light pure enough to see them.*

Lily and I are cool. We didn't talk about it, but she's not upset with me anymore—whatever it was, she let it go. She gave me a heartfelt hug and thanked me for taking such good care of her.

We ate dessert by the fire and lay around and talked and I didn't want to leave, until I thought of my adorable pink home.

Ingy fell asleep against her mom in a black lace bundle, and Claudia and I loaded her into the backseat of the wagon and covered her with a blanket. We kissed the two East Oakland angels goodbye, and I drove us home: the 880 to the 580 to the 24, and down MLK.

December 1

In the box Clara sent was a bunch of stuff I was collecting and making for Willow:

1. six beautiful Japanese fabrics I was going to make her a quilt with
2. soft, furry brown hoodie with bear ears on top, size 0-3 months
3. gingham diaper covers in red, blue, and gray
4. adorable stuffed seafoam-green baby elephant
5. Guatemalan baby ankle bracelet with bells, from Sean's trip there

I dropped off the box on Asha and Terra's new porch, with a note saying "You two are going to make a beautiful baby."

December 8

July understood love. She got it, she was good at it. She was showing me how to do it right. Not like my rabid love for Dani, or my half-ass love for Sean, but a good, unconditional love.

I threw it away, my love. I had a real love and I sent her away.

I miss her. I miss her terribly. My body feels weird without her, wrong.

Maybe all those couples putting up with good-enough are smarter than I am. Maybe the pieces that are good in a relationship are enough to suck on when things aren't great. Maybe I should have focused on our good rather than shining a light where we were broken.

"You are worth every bad date I ever had. I have been waiting my whole life for you."

This is what she said to me.

I wonder if she's still waiting.

December 13

Sean called today. He wanted to know what I'm doing for the holidays and I thought about inviting him up here for Christmas, so I don't end up alone.

But he's got family obligations down there. And that's not who we are anymore.

He did, however, say he'll go get Moonshine from my parents next year and bring him to me.

I know he's worried about me. But it's not his job to fix it.

It's my job, taking care of me. It's all I have to do now. Though I do need some income very soon.

Maybe I will go back to school, for that mythical MFA in Creative Writing, after all.

December 21

4:49 a.m.

Winter solstice. Shortest day of the year. End of darkness, beginning of light. I want to be up for all of it.

I've been sitting at my desk remembering when I first came to this house, almost a year ago. All of us dreaming of a perfect world.

I realized that every time I sat at my desk to write, I was facing out onto July's room, as though I dreamt her up with my words. Finding what you're searching for right outside your window, that's gotta be some kind of miracle.

Oh, my god—just as I was looking over there, a tiny baby raccoon popped out of the folds of the palm tree. And then another, and another, until there were six of them, and finally their mother. Now I'm sitting here grinning at their tiny little faces, just a few feet away from me. I opened my window and they're squeaking little Good Mornings into the pinkening light.

It's been a very long time since I've been up at dawn. Never in this house. All those insomnia nights, I was always so focused on getting back to sleep at dawn, I never got up and looked out. Maybe I slept through whole litters growing up right outside my window.

I wish we could fly, the raccoon babies and I, just float around in the clouds, which are just now showing in the sky above their tree. There were a few times, in those early days, when I lost my way, found the palm tree in the sky, and followed it home.

July could see the raccoons too, from her room. I wonder if she ever has. I feel like I need to show her, before they're gone forever, grown up and moved away. Otherwise I'll always wonder if it was all just a dream.

The whole time I've lived here, I've been looking inside the house for everything, but just outside my window is a whole other world.

I'm watching the light fill my room, fill the whole sky, melt the clouds. The raccoons went back into the palm tree to sleep the day away. I wish I could climb out onto it and across to July's, without my feet ever touching the ground. I want to be carried by the light of the morning, want to carry it over to her, into her.

5:55. I'm pretty sure Sweet Adeline opens at 6. I'll get some stuff and bring it to her.

And I know how I'll tell her the truth, finally. I'll let her read this journal. It's been for her all along.

10:47 p.m.
Sadie just got back from July's. She was there all day.

At 6:10, I went to July's house and knocked on her window. I was awkwardly carrying two coffees and a ched-dar chive scone, a chocolate chip cookie, and a slice of sun-dried tomato quiche.

She got up and let me in. I followed her into her room, where she climbed back in bed and glared at me over the covers. She wasn't wearing her glasses and I was afraid to go too close.

I asked her if she would be willing to read something that would explain everything.

She waited what seemed like a long time, perfectly still, her eyes on me. And then she nodded.

I pulled Sadie out and onto her bed, opened this docu-ment to the first page. I set the food and her coffee on her bedside table and left.

When I got back home I had no Sadie to play with and a

ton of nervous energy, wired on coffee in the early morning.

I rolled around on the carpet for a while, did some butoh.

I carved my initials in the armoire. At the top. I used Asha's orange ceramic knife, which she either forgot or left for me because she knows I love it.

An N for Nara and an S for Sara, with a heart around them. I heart myself.

Then I cleaned the house. Dusted and vacuumed both floors, scrubbed the kitchen and bathroom, scrubbed myself.

When I got out of the bath and came out of the downstairs bathroom, out of the corner of my eye I caught a flash of red.

Sadie was sitting on the top stair, like she'd just walked in. I had totally forgotten that July had a house key.

The file was open to the last page, with this addition at the end:

> What a sad story. I'll be next door trying to decide if it deserves a happy ending.
>
> Love,
> July

Now I'm sitting at the top of the stairs, in my kimono, imagining her sitting at the top of her steps in her yellow T-shirt. Trying to pull her back to me.

Please, July, forgive me. Please, please forgive me.

Maybe I should go over there. What if she's going home for the holidays? She could be leaving any minute for D.C. Fuck.

July, July, please please please forgive me.

I'm going over there. I'll ask her if I can give her a kiss. One kiss that will make everything right again.

I have to fight for us. This can't be the end of our love story.

I went up to the attic and put on the gold lamé dress I was wearing when we first kissed, in front of the Alcatraz Liquor Store. I didn't bother with makeup, just put on a hoodie and pulled the hood up over my wet hair.

It's dark outside. The end of the beginning of light. I was awake for all of it.

I think I'm finished reporting this story. I don't need it anymore. It was the words that cured me, in the end.

These 68,679 words were my dosage for the year, better than Vicodin, Xanax, or Oxy.

Black stars on a white sky. All I had to do was follow them here.

Arigato to:

Dagmar Miura
Ocean Mandela Milan
Kali Steele
Hisae Matsuda
Tiana Krahn
Michelle Eigen
Quinton Zachary Watson
Gregory Slay
Brian from Missoula
Christopher Church
Leah Morrison
Katia Noyes
Becca Lee
Britt Sutton
Tammy Stoner
Julia Nowak
Erika Larsen
Sue Kim
Elizabeth Hollis Hansen
Brook Pieri
Kelly Stone
Jonathan Merrill
Kristy Lin Billuni
Shivaun Nestor
Noah Kopp
Jen Leland